"Sebastian, I'm hardly a child."

"I never said you were," he protested. "But you're scarcely worldly. You remind me of a rose about to open. You're full of promise. Megan, why are you so afraid of finding the love you've dreamed about—maybe with me?"

How wonderful his words made her feel! But she was so confused...

"You're a threat to me because I enjoy being self-sufficient. I don't want to lose that sense of being my own person. I've worked so hard to get it!" She paused, then added, "To you, I'm different. You've admitted that's partly why you're attracted to me. What happens when you grow used to me?"

"I'm drawn to you because of who you are, not just because you're different. You're beautiful, Megan, but also sensitive. There's a vulnerability about you that makes me want to take you in my arms. I don't want anyone or anything to hurt you. I just want to be with you. Is that so wrong?"

"No, it's not so wrong," she said, barely audibly...

Dear Reader:

We're celebrating SECOND CHANCE AT LOVE's third birthday with a new cover format! I'm sure you had no trouble recognizing our traditional butterfly logo and distinctive SECOND CHANCE AT LOVE type. But you probably also noticed that the cover artwork is considerably larger than before. We're thrilled with the new look, and we hope you are, too!

In a sense, our new cover treatment reflects what's been happening *inside* SECOND CHANCE AT LOVE books. We're constantly striving to bring you fresh and original romances with unexpected twists and delightful surprises. We introduce promising new writers on a regular basis. And we aim for variety by publishing some romances that are funny, some that are poignant, some that are "traditional," and some that take an entirely new approach. SECOND CHANCE AT LOVE is constantly evolving to meet your need for "something new" in your romance reading.

At the same time, we *haven't* changed the successful editorial concept behind each SECOND CHANCE AT LOVE romance. And we've consistently maintained a reputation for being a line of the highest quality.

So, just like the new covers, SECOND CHANCE AT LOVE romances are satisfyingly familiar—yet excitingly different—and better than ever!

Happy reading,

Ellen Edwards

Ellen Edwards, Senior Editor
SECOND CHANCE AT LOVE
The Berkley Publishing Group
200 Madison Avenue
New York, N.Y. 10016

P.S.   Do you receive our SECOND CHANCE AT LOVE and TO HAVE AND TO HOLD newsletter? If not, be sure to fill out the coupon in the back of this book, and we'll send you the newsletter free of charge four times a year.

Second Chance at Love®

ONE MORE TOMORROW

AIMÉE DUVALL

A SECOND CHANCE AT LOVE
BOOK

Other Second Chance at Love books by
Aimée Duvall

ONE MORE TOMORROW

First edition published August 1984

First printing

"Second Chance at Love" and the butterfly emblem are trademarks belonging to Jove Publications, Inc.

Printed in the United States of America

Second Chance at Love books are published by
The Berkley Publishing Group
200 Madison Avenue, New York, NY 10016

To the real Megan Lord, for all the help and for being such a good sport; to John T., for memories of dragons in military uniform and for teaching me that teddy bears can have claws; and to Lynn Stanek, for showing me that tall blondes can be as insecure as stubby, dark-haired authors.

Acknowledgments

With special thanks to Helen Aragon, of Helen's Hallmark Shop; to Jeff Bruch, for the guided tour of San Francisco; and to Norm Parrish, of SCORE Chapter 67.

CHAPTER ONE

As an impeccably attired butler held out a silver serving tray, Megan Lord selected a tall tulip-shaped champagne glass filled to the brim with pale, bubbling liquid. Smiling politely, she then turned her attention back to the other formally dressed guests gathered around the oval pool of their new landlord's luxurious home in the Presidio Terrace district of San Francisco.

Her little gift shop, Off the Beaten Path, would probably fit on the owner's front lawn, Megan thought, awed by the beautiful gardens and impressive town house. Indeed, the estate was unusual for the city, where even the most expensive homes rarely included much land.

Most of the other businesspeople present, all of whom also rented space in the shopping center owned by Sebastian Gladstone, their host, looked as apprehensive as Megan felt. But, despite the old adage that misery loves company, the observation didn't make her feel any better.

Megan smiled as Emma King approached. The middle-aged lady ran the antique shop next to Megan's store, and she looked stylishly chic in a rose-colored cocktail dress and pearls. Mrs. King was known to be quite well off, and usually referred to her business as her "dear little hobby."

"Hello, Mrs. King. Isn't it a beautiful evening?" Megan greeted her. "It's so warm for this time of year." Megan hadn't attended many really fancy parties and had a limited repertoire of conversational topics available to her, but the weather was always a safe subject.

"Oh, please call me Emma," the woman enthused. "After all, we're shopping-mall neighbors." She let out a tinkling laugh. "The weather has been lovely the last few days. Why, just the other night my dear husband, Edgar, and I went for a drive in his sports car after attending the opening of *La Sylphide*. The coast was magnificent. As busy as you are, do you ever get to the theater?"

Megan smiled vacantly, trying to remember the last time she'd been to a movie. She certainly hadn't seen the la whatever Mrs. King had referred to. "I certainly admire your patience, Emma," she said, "but I just can't sit through those foreign films myself. The subtitles are so distracting, I usually can't follow the action. My roommate and I recently saw *Revenge of the Zombies*, an English classic, at a revival house. It was actually a very good movie."

Emma King regarded her quizzically, then broke into gentle laughter. "Why, Megan, I do believe you're putting me on. It's easy to see where you get all the amusing ideas for your little shop. Nevertheless, someday you must attend the ballet with me. I'll let Edgar have a night with his friends at the club while you and I enjoy an evening on the town. We'll have a great time."

Embarrassed by her faux pas, Megan managed a weak "Thank you" as the woman excused herself and drifted over to another circle of guests. How could she have been such an idiot? Megan berated herself. Emma King had been talking about the ballet, not a movie!

Well, how could she have known? Megan thought miserably. The only ballet she had ever seen was the *Nutcracker* on television. Of course she had heard of *Swan Lake* and a few others, but where she came from, music was made by fiddles and banjos, and the only dance was the two-step. Maybe she should get out more often. San Francisco was supposed to have all the cultural opportunities anyone could ever want, but she was too poor and too busy to take advantage of them.

Searching for a familiar face, Megan spotted her roommate Erin, looking poised and confident on her way back from the buffet table. She handed Megan a tiny plate heaped with food. "You look absolutely sensational in that dress," Erin exclaimed. "That silvery-blue color exactly matches your eyes."

"Thanks," Megan said, some of her self-confidence restored. She accepted the plate with a smile. "And thanks for buying this dress for my twenty-sixth birthday. It's the most beautiful outfit I've ever owned." The chiffon and taffeta gown with its handkerchief hemline looked very chic. The sheer overlay created a draped cowl neckline that merged softly with the split-cape sleeves.

"You haven't bought anything new in ages," Erin said, "but when I saw that dress, I knew it would be perfect for you. Now you don't look like the girl next door."

Megan cringed, hating the description that people had used to describe her for as far back as she could remember. Her shoulder-length blond hair, the smattering of freckles that dotted her nose, and her scant use of makeup made her look so all-American that people were constantly commenting on the fact. Her San Franciscan friends

teased her by calling her "wholesome." Still, after spending eighteen months in the city, she saw no reason to
make any major changes in her appearance. She was
happy being herself—except, of course, at embarrassing
moments like the one with Mrs. King. At times like those
she truly envied Erin's sophistication.

Erin's willowy frame, ebony hair, and dark-brown
eyes gave her an exotic allure. Even her nails were long,
beautiful, and polished a deep scarlet. Megan glanced at
her own wide, stubby nails and sighed.

"Earth calling, Megan. Are you daydreaming again?"
Erin's teasing tone brought Megan out of her reverie. "I
don't know what to do with you. How you've managed
to pass puberty and still look so innocent is beyond me."

"I don't see it as an asset, myself," Megan argued.
"I think my looks are so average they're boring." With
a sharp jab she speared an olive studded with something
red she didn't recognize and consumed it greedily. Whatever these hors d'oeuvres were, they tasted great. She
picked up a yellow one shaped like a rose, thinking it
must be a mint, and bit down on it. "Ugh! This is awful!
It tastes like butter!"

Erin laughed loudly. "It *is* butter, you ninny! Haven't
you ever seen molded butter?"

Megan washed out her mouth with several quick gulps
of champagne. "Butter? Good grief! Why would anyone
mold pats of butter into flower shapes? To save my soul,
I can't imagine anyone taking a lump of that stuff and
trying to make a sculpture out of it!"

"Welcome to the big city," Erin said, chuckling. "I
put that butter there for the piece of sourdough bread still
on your plate."

Megan grimaced and glanced surreptitiously around
the room before meeting her friend's gaze. "I feel so out
of place here! My kind of party is an outdoor barbecue.
I'm just not suited for this type of thing." With some

embarrassment Megan described her conversation with Mrs. King.

Erin laughed. *"La Sylphide* is a *ballet."*

Megan rolled her eyes. "I know that now."

"You're lucky you're so pretty," Erin said, "or people would probably insult you instead of thinking it's cute when you say silly things."

"I know I'm not as cosmopolitan as you are," Megan said defensively, "but for the first time in my life I'm making my own decisions. I make mistakes, too, but at least now I'm in control of my life."

She thought back to the events of the past year and a half. Just knowing she could make it on her own sent an incredible rush of satisfaction through her. With the money she had saved during her ten-month stint as a sales clerk in San Francisco's largest department store, and her small divorce settlement, she had been able to open Off the Beaten Path and realize her dream of becoming financially self-supporting and independent.

She still remembered how, until just a few months ago, she'd collapsed in bed each night after working double shifts at the store. She'd often wondered if all her effort was really worth it. But then she recalled her life in the small town of Ironton, Missouri, where she'd been a sales clerk in her aunt's small dress shop. Year in and year out, she had worked long, hard hours, gaining experience but never acquiring the sense of accomplishment or satisfaction that came from working toward a goal of your own choosing.

Even in retrospect her past seemed filled with pain. Life had never been easy for her. Her parents had died in an automobile accident when she was fourteen, and she'd been sent to live with her maiden aunt, a charitable woman but not a warm one. Megan had found her aunt's strict rules of conduct unbearably repressive. What's more, even her marriage had been a failure from the beginning.

She'd traveled a long, rough journey to be where she was today.

She was proud of what she'd accomplished. Despite the difficulties, she had succeeded in making a life for herself. Equally important, she had proven she had the intelligence and determination to make her dream of owning her own store come true.

She didn't delude herself into thinking her financial difficulties were over. After all, Off the Beaten Path was only four months old and far from an overnight success.

What if, instead of barely breaking even, the store had been a smash hit from the very first and she'd gone instantly from rags to riches? For a brief moment she envisioned herself walking out onto this crowded terrace like a grande dame of the retail business. She pictured herself chatting graciously with everyone around her, acting charming and sophisticated. Suddenly she'd come face to face with Sebastian Gladstone, the owner of the shopping center, who, it was rumored, was going to increase their rent. Immediately captivated by her incredible beauty and feminine allure, he would announce to one and all that, at her request, he had reconsidered and decided that a rent increase would not be necessary after all. In her imagination everyone turned to her in grateful admiration and lavished her with praise.

Megan was startled out of her daydream by Erin saying, "We might as well take a seat." She gestured toward a couple of empty chairs. "I understand our host's flight arrived late from L. A. and that he got here just a few minutes ago."

"I really hope there's no truth to the rumor that he plans to increase everyone's rent," Megan whispered. "I can't afford to pay one more dime."

"If you don't mind a little bit of sage advice from your shop's smallest but only investor," Erin said seriously, "if Sebastian Gladstone raises the rent, I think you should pay it. I can help out with my paycheck from the radio station." She held up a hand to stem Megan's protests. "Keep in mind that with all the new construction under way in that area of town, as well as the nightclubs and restaurants moving into the district, the shopping center's location is going to be darn near perfect in terms of accessibility to the public."

"I know." Megan sipped her champagne slowly. "But to tell you the truth, I'm hoping to present Mr. Gladstone with an alternate business proposition. The problem is I'm not sure what type of deal to offer, since I don't know anything about him."

"Maybe I can help. I've been reading the society page ever since I arrived here, four years ago. The Gladstones own the largest vineyard in California, so they're usually prominently featured. From what I remember reading, Sebastian refused to stay in the family wine business. I don't recall all the details, but in the end his father settled with Sebastian by giving him an enormous sum of money, then ordered him to leave home. For a year and a half Sebastian played the stock market and made other investments quite skillfully. Rumor has it that he doubled his money. Then, about three months ago, he began reinvesting everything he'd made. According to the gossip columnists, if all his deals turn out the way he hopes, and who knows how much he's made already, his wealth will far exceed his father's."

Megan was impressed. "Wow. He must be either brave or very foolhardy. Investing your last penny in anything, regardless of how good the deal, is a nerve-wracking proposition. Take it from me, I know." She turned her attention to the various dishes spread out on the buffet table. "I'm going to get myself a couple of sandwiches. Can I bring you back something?"

Erin shook her head. "No, I'm going to mingle. You never can tell. Maybe I'll learn something interesting about our host and his plans for this evening."

"I've already tried making small talk," Megan replied. "I think I'll stick to something I'm really good at—like eating."

As Erin laughed, Megan strolled over to the buffet table, where she filled her plate with assorted cold cuts and sweets. But when she tried to return to her chair, she found a small, boisterous group of guests blocking her way. Trying to get around them, she stepped onto the pool's tile-covered edging and carefully navigated the narrow strip between the group of guests and the deep pool. Taking one careful step at a time, she held her heaped plate with one hand, holding out her other arm to maintain her balance. She was almost around the laughing, jostling group when a tall blond man wearing a dark tuxedo backed unexpectedly into her.

His solid back rammed against her shoulder and sent her plate of food flying into the air, scattering the contents around her. An involuntary cry was wrenched from her lips as she felt her feet slipping out from under her. In the next instant she was tumbling uncontrollably over the edge of the pool and into the warm, chlorine-scented depths.

Thank God she remembered to keep her eyes closed! With a furious kicking of arms and legs, she forced her way to the surface, gasping for breath, and grasped the concrete edge. Cautiously she opened her eyes. Relief! Her contact lenses were still in place; she could see. But in her mad fall she'd lost a shoe, which was even now drifting to the bottom of the pool, and her once-beautiful dress had become a sodden mass of twisted, ruined chiffon tangled around her waist and legs. Her blond hair was plastered to her head like a helmet and hung in clotted strands.

All at once she realized that the startled gasps of the crowd had given way to gentle laughter. "Oh!" she exclaimed, humiliated beyond belief. It was the most embarrassing moment of her life! How could such a terrible thing be happening to her?

She had to get control of herself and climb out of the pool as gracefully as possible. With renewed determination, she searched desperately for a means of escape—and found herself staring into the bluest eyes she'd ever seen, set in a ruggedly handsome male face that could have come straight out of her wildest fantasy. He was kneeling at the edge of the pool, apparently oblivious to the danger posed to his immaculate black tuxedo by the roiling pool water. She stared speechless as he reached out a hand and, in a surprisingly gentle gesture, pushed a dripping strand of hair out of her eyes and away from her cheeks. His strong palm cupped the side of her face in a brief caress that set her pulse pounding. His eyes were warm, with crinkling laugh lines that hinted at his suppressed amusement.

"I realize this evening's very warm for early September," he said, "but haven't you picked a rather drastic way to cool off?"

For a brief moment she couldn't answer. Time seemed to stand still as she continued to stare into the aquamarine eyes poised above her. Nothing in her experience had prepared her for the devastating impact of his warm look and tender touch. Despite the chill beginning to creep into her, she felt enveloped in warmth, breathless from his nearness. Finally she found her voice. "Someone knocked into me," she said lamely, wishing she could vanish into thin air.

"That was my fault, I'm afraid." He took her hand and held it in a firm grip. "I'll be happy to pay for any damages to your beautiful dress, but I can't honestly say I'm sorry. You look gorgeous. With a few changes here and there, you'd make a perfect mermaid."

"Just help me out of here, please," she mumbled miserably. "I don't need compliments. I need a life preserver."

"Come now, be a good sport. It's a lovely night for a swim." His eyes appraised the swell of her breasts, lingering on the outline of her taut nipples beneath the thin dress. In a soft voice he added, "Water, it seems, has no detrimental effect on your appearance. In fact, I think it enhances it." He clasped her other hand in a firm grip and began to lift her out of the pool.

She tried to make it easier for him by bracing her feet against the concrete wall and pushing upward. The tiles were slippery, but she was sure they could make it. With one last push—"Ugh!" she cried out as both feet slipped at once, and she fell backward with sudden force, jerking her "savior" off his feet and headfirst into the pool!

He landed practically on top of her, with a mighty splash that sent a wave of water careening over the side. With a startled gasp the guests rushed backward, out of harm's way, then forward again to view Megan and her companion as, kicking and thrashing, they attempted to disentangle their arms and legs and swim to safety. Boisterous laughter that was very inappropriate to the refined setting echoed across the terrace.

Megan's tuxedoed companion wiped water from his face, consternation and amusement warring in his expression. "Did you *have* to do that?" he demanded.

"I'm so sorry," she exclaimed. "I really am! I had no idea that would happen. I really didn't do it on purpose. It was as much an accident as when you knocked me in!"

"That *was* an accident," he retorted.

"That's what I said!" She must be on the verge of hysteria, she concluded miserably. Taking a deep breath, she forced herself to look at him. His shoulders were as wide as a football player's. His angular face was intriguingly handsome, his aquamarine eyes mesmerizing, his softly curling blond hair slightly darkened by the water. The thick path of chest hair just visible beneath his soaked white shirt added to his masculine appeal.

"Admit it," he teased, his anger apparently dissipating. "You just wanted to get a closer look at me. What better way than to get me as wet as you are?"

Her stomach felt weighted with lead, and she knew that the attention of every person within earshot was riveted on her. Tense silence descended. Fury and mortification battled within her. How dare he taunt her!

Saying nothing, instead shooting her companion a look meant to wither steel, she accepted the hand offered by Charlie Rivers, the owner of the clock shop just down the hall from her store. In one smooth motion he took her outreached arms and lifted her almost effortlessly from the pool. Megan thanked Charlie and stood shakily by the side of the pool, her arms clutched tightly over her breasts, as several other guests helped the blond man out of the water.

Megan looked down at herself in dismay. "Oh, my new dress!" she cried. She slipped off her remaining shoe, gathered together the sodden folds of her gown, and wrung a stream of water from the ruined material. A small pool formed at her feet.

Just then, Erin ran up and handed Megan her purse. "Here. You're lucky you left it on the chair when you got up. I'll go back to the apartment and bring you some dry clothes. Until then, why don't you go inside and dry off? If you stay out here, you'll end up with pneumonia."

To Megan's relief, the butler hurried over carrying a large bath towel, which he draped over her shoulders. "That's good advice, miss. We can put you upstairs until your friend returns with your clothing. In the meantime, I'll retrieve your shoe from the pool."

Megan started to decline, but changed her mind abruptly as a chilling breeze whipped against her. Erin was right. If she didn't dry off soon, she was bound to end up sick. With murmured words of thanks, she followed the butler through thick sliding glass doors into a broad entrance hall.

The high white ceiling was supported by enormous matching pillars, and the walls were covered with a shiny black fabric. A gold and black oriental trunk stood in the center of the oak floor along with several chairs and end tables, all upholstered in gold cloth trimmed with midnight-blue bands. Flowering plants stood in ornate planters, and the staircase toward which she moved was white, the steps richly carpeted in black with gold bands.

Megan just reached the stairs when the handsome perpetrator of her mishap, clad in wet trousers with a large towel instead of his jacket covering his shoulders, emerged from another entrance. "That's okay, Williams," he said. "I'll show the young lady the way."

Megan faced him angrily. "Please, just go away and leave me alone! It's bad enough that, thanks to you, I've made a complete fool out of myself. Must you keep reminding me of it by insisting on helping me?"

He didn't quite succeed in suppressing a grin. "No woman as lovely as you are has any reason to be embarrassed by her appearance, regardless of the circumstances," he said gallantly.

Avoiding his eyes, Megan stared at her soaked, stockinged feet. Maybe if she wished it hard enough, the earth would open up and swallow her whole. "If you'll point me in the right direction, I'll be glad to leave you to your own attempts to dry off."

He shook his head. "I insist on taking you upstairs and making sure you have everything you need. I'll even let you use my bedroom. It has a large mirrored dressing area I think you'll find useful."

Megan started to tell him that he needn't bother when a sudden realization brought her to an abrupt halt. *"You're*

Sebastian Gladstone?" she asked in disbelief.

He nodded. "You have the advantage over me, I'm afraid."

"I'm Megan Lord." To her horror she realized she had stammered out the words. Hating herself for allowing her nervousness to show, she straightened her back and regarded him levelly.

It was impossible not to feel drawn by the mesmeric intensity of his heavy-lidded gaze. Something in his stance attested to his awareness of the masculine power he held over her. He frowned briefly as he considered her name. "Mee-gan? That's an unusual way to pronounce your name."

"It's the Welsh pronunciation. My mother was of Welsh extraction," she explained. "The more common pronunciation, Maygan, is Irish. And, of course, the Irish outnumber the Welsh, so..."

"I see your point," he said, laughing. "You know, this is going to sound like a line, but your name sounds familiar. Have we met before?"

Megan shook her head. "No. I would have remembered someone like you." To her chagrin, the revealing words were out before she could stop them.

But, to her surprise, he didn't seem angry. His teeth flashed in a smile. "There's no way I would have forgotten you, either."

Her cheeks grew hot under his steady scrutiny. If only she had Erin's sophistication; Erin would know how to handle this situation. Perhaps she should take lessons from her roommate.

Unable to will herself to look directly at him, Megan feigned great interest in the stair railing while studying Sebastian Gladstone out of the corner of her eye. Even with a towel wrapped around his upper body, he exuded a dignity appropriate to his background.

Suddenly comprehension shone in his eyes. "You own

Off the Beaten Path, don't you?" he said. "Ever since I heard about your store, I've been wanting to meet you."

"There are certainly easier ways of doing that than by knocking me into the pool," she said dryly.

He laughed. The sound was rich and vibrant, with a throaty timbre that sparked a wealth of sensations within her. "I gather I've been forgiven."

Remembering who he was and what was at stake— the survival of her store and her own livelihood—she tried to block out the sensual awareness his presence evoked. "Why don't we make a trade?" she suggested. "I'll forgive you for any past and/or future transgressions if you'll promise not to raise the rent, as it's rumored around the shopping center you plan to do."

His expression grew serious. "I'm afraid that's one promise I can't make."

Her heart constricted. There was no way she could pay for a rent increase from her store's meager profits. An increase would mean the end of her store—and of the dream that had sustained her ever since leaving Missouri. But she refused to give up. There must be a reasonable compromise they could make. She wouldn't let this wealthy, intensely handsome man cause everything she had worked for during the past year and a half to come tumbling down around her. This wasn't the time to let her attraction to him intimidate her.

Should she try to reach him on a personal level, one human being to another? She discarded the thought. How could she make someone who had obviously never worried where his next meal was coming from, or if he could pay the rent, understand what it was like to live on her tight budget?

She had to account for every penny she spent. There was never enough money to cover all the bills—a problem that had grown worse since she'd opened the store.

Every dime went back into the business in one form or another.

She had long ago given up the small luxuries other people took for granted, like seeing an occasional movie or going out for dinner.

Her one luxury, such as it was, came from her spare change in a large mason jar. At the end of the month she took it all out and counted it. If the total came to a dollar, she rewarded herself with two eclairs from her favorite bakery. More often than not, however, that amount never materialized. She had to rob the jar frequently for bus fare and odds and ends from the grocery store, leaving precious little by the end of the month.

As Megan accompanied Sebastian Gladstone up the stairs of his town house, she asked, "So, tell me what you've heard about my store that made you want to meet me."

A devilish gleam shone in his eyes. "Let's slip into some dry clothes first. Then I'll tell you all about it." He led her to the master bedroom and, going directly to the closet, selected a pair of gray pants, a pale-blue shirt, and a navy sports coat. "I have a pair of jeans that might fit you," he ventured, studying her figure with undisguised appreciation. "You'll find them on a hook next to the shower."

"I appreciate the offer of jeans, but I won't need them," she said. "Erin should be here in about twenty minutes or so with my own clothes. It'll take me that long to shower, dry off, and fix myself up again."

"All right. In the meantime I'm going down the hall to change, then downstairs to announce the rent increase. I don't expect to be terribly popular tonight, but the job's got to be done. To bring in enough income to show an acceptable profit, I have to increase the shopping center leasing charges. If you like, I'll spare you having to rush downstairs before you're ready by telling you now what I plan to do."

At her nod, he took a deep breath. "Basically, I intend to spend a lot of money advertising the center on radio, television, and in the newspapers. Charging a higher rent will allow me to do that. If everything goes smoothly, we should begin to draw in more customers immediately. Paying more for rent might inconvenience some people, but in the long run we'll all profit. It's the only way I can stay in business right now."

Inconvenience? If only he knew! "I see," Megan said stiffly.

"Take my word for it. If you decide not to relocate your store, you'll enjoy a sharp upswing in business."

Megan didn't doubt that for a minute. But that didn't alter the fact that her store's profits were too small to cover any extra expenses. She needed to bargain with Sebastian. But what could she offer him as a suitable trade-off?

He crossed the bedroom and gestured toward a dressing room. "There are lots of clean towels behind the mirrored door. Feel free to use any of my things until yours arrive." He grabbed a comb from the dresser top and walked out, closing the door behind him.

Megan took a quick shower and entered the dressing area as she finished toweling herself dry. After wrapping a dry towel around her, securing it just above her breasts, she sat down on a chair, vigorously rubbed her soaked head, and carefully combed out her hair. Finally she returned to the bedroom.

It felt odd to be in a stranger's bedroom, practically naked, but she had little choice until Erin arrived. Her eyes burned from the chlorine. At least, she had managed to hold onto her contact lenses. Eager to remove them for a few minutes and give her eyes a rest, she searched her purse for the lens case. She couldn't find it. Damn!

She slumped dejectedly onto the bed. Of all the rotten luck.

A light knock sounded on the door. "Who is it?"

"It's Erin. Are you decent?"

"Yes, come on in."

The statuesque brunette entered carrying a small overnight case and the shoe that had fallen in the pool. "I brought everything from a curling iron to my lilac jumpsuit. The butler fished your shoe from the pool."

"Your jumpsuit? Why didn't you pick something from my closet?"

Erin smiled smugly. "Because this is the sexiest outfit I own, and I'd sure like to see you put it to good use."

"Wait a minute. This isn't the one with the V-neck opening that reaches to the waist, is it?" Megan asked in dismay.

Erin nodded happily. "You'll drive all the men wild. Especially *him.*"

"I don't think so," Megan said resolutely. "I'm putting my soggy dress back on and going home."

"Oh no, you're not."

"Oh yes, I am." But before Megan could stop her, Erin had scooped up the dress and was running to the door. In another instant she had ducked out into the hall. "Erin, come back here!" Megan took off after her friend, but as she rounded the bed, she struck her big toe on a bedpost and collapsed as a sharp pain shot up her shin. "Augh!" she cried, adding one of her rare but heartfelt curses. She dropped onto the mattress with a groan, raising her foot to her lap. She tried to massage away the pain. The toe was red and throbbing, but she had to admit it didn't seem to be severely damaged.

"Erin, you traitor, come back here!" Megan called out angrily. When her friend failed to reappear, she shouted, "I know you're out there!" She listened. Silence. "You gloomy ghoul, I hope you go prematurely bald! I hope you're cursed with chronic anxiety about the weather. If you didn't have the backbone of a chocolate eclair, you'd get in here and fight!"

Megan waited, slumped in defeat. Mumbling angrily to herself, she trailed her fingers lightly over the smooth lilac material of her roommate's outfit. Maybe she should try on the jumpsuit and see how it looked. After all, if Erin could wear something like this, why couldn't she?

Just then, Erin opened the door a crack and peered inside, flashing a mischievous grin. "By the way, I left your car right where you parked it. One of the guys offered to give me a ride home, so I won't need it. Have fun!"

Megan groaned loudly and tossed a soaked shoe at Erin, who slammed the door shut just before the projectile bounced harmlessly onto the carpeted floor.

Megan closed her eyes and sighed. Maybe this change of events was for the best. She was very attracted to Sebastian, and seeing her dressed in her usual skirt and blouse would hardly have set his heart on fire. She shook her head. How could she hope to truly interest a man like Sebastian Gladstone? She wasn't part of the society in-crowd he had grown up with. Once he saw her as she really was, he'd probably become utterly bored.

What could they possibly talk about? She couldn't imagine he'd be enthralled by her Missouri hometown's most interesting story—about the time when all the cows from John Mathews' dairy had strayed into the onion patch and given the town's milk a very distinct flavor for several days.

Megan gave Erin's jumpsuit a second speculative glance. Maybe she *should* try the seductive look. It wouldn't hurt to try to appear more sophisticated around Sebastian Gladstone. She could consider it a test of her acting ability, a chance to see if she could carry off such a ruse.

Without hesitating further, she slipped into the outfit. It felt fine on her—maybe a little more revealing around the bosom than she was used to, but that was the point, or wasn't it?

As Megan put on her makeup, she tried not to hold back on the lipstick and eye shadow, attempting to create a look closer to Erin's. She studied her reflection in the mirror. She had to admit she looked more exotic now. She stepped back to see in the full-length mirror. Not bad!

Afraid her resolve would weaken, Megan hurried out of the bedroom, closing the door behind her. She took a deep breath, trying to gather up her courage, and then walked sedately down the stairs.

The foyer below her was empty. So was the terrace visible through the sliding glass doors. Surprised, she stared openmouthed. Before she had a chance to recover, Sebastian entered from another room and let out a low whistle. "You look sensational!"

A warm flush crept over her face. Her stomach felt as if she had swallowed a bucket of concrete and the mixture was starting to solidify inside her. "Thanks."

"Shall we go into the den and have a drink?"

She nodded. "Where did everyone go?"

Sebastian sighed. "I don't think they felt much like partying after I made my announcement. But their response wasn't completely unfavorable. After everyone has had a chance to consider my proposals, I think they'll see that my idea will profit all of us."

Not everyone, Megan thought glumly. Only those who could pay the price. Her throat tightened. "Actually, I could use a drink," she decided.

"Certainly."

They entered a large wood-paneled den. Megan took a seat on a leather sofa across from Sebastian's desk. Two of the four walls were covered with bookcases, one of them housing leather-bound volumes with bright gold lettering.

"What would you like?" Sebastian asked from behind the bar.

What would someone sophisticated drink in this situation? Megan wondered. Would a particular drink go well with the outfit she was wearing? Unable to think of anything, and knowing he was waiting for an answer, she blurted out, "A glass of white wine, please." Terrific. That was about as original as a jelly doughnut.

"Coming up."

She watched him as he walked to the bar. "Mr. Gladstone—" she began.

"Call me Sebastian," he interrupted.

"All right." She inhaled deeply, trying to gather her courage. "Sebastian, my store has been open only a short time, just four months."

"I know. I've seen some of the ads you've run in the newspaper. Off the Beaten Path sounds like an interesting place. I love your idea of selling ungreeting cards. A friend of mine sent me the one that says, 'I'm having a miserable time on my vacation. I lost my luggage and my wallet, and I can't drink the water. Wish you were here.' Ever since then I've been wanting to pay Off the Beaten Path a visit. I just had to meet the lady who owns that shop."

Megan laughed nervously, then forced herself to be serious. "The ungreeting cards got my store off to a good start, but I'm far from reaching my financial goals. I can't afford a rent increase right now, but I would agree to give you a percentage of my net profits."

"All the stores already pay seven percent of their gross to the corporate owners, in addition to their rent. That's standard practice across the country. What are you offering me that I don't already get?"

Megan braced herself. She had to convince him somehow, to appeal to him in a purely logical, businesslike manner. She leaned back in her chair as she weighed her words.

Sebastian brought a platter of sandwiches to the sofa. He offered her one, then helped himself before setting the plate on the coffee table. Automatically, she picked up half a chicken salad sandwich and took a small bite. "How about if I offer you two percent of my net, in addition to what you already receive of the gross, for the first six months? My business is growing rapidly, and of course the more I make, the larger your two percent profit will become. After six months I'll also begin to pay the rent increase, while you continue to collect your two percent until the lease expires a year from now."

Megan had just finished making her proposal when she felt a speck of dirt in her eye. The irritating particle was too small to cause a torrential flood of tears, but it was annoying nevertheless. Lowering her eyelids, she rolled her eyes, hoping to dislodge the speck as unobtrusively as possible. Nonchalantly she gently touched the inner corner and fluttered her lashes. Sometimes that was all it took to relieve the discomfort.

But not this time. As Sebastian excused himself and returned to the bar, Megan again touched her eyelid gently. Suddenly her contact lens popped out, and the world became a kaleidoscope of sharp and fuzzy images in a crazy collage of colors!

Oh, horrors! What was she supposed to do now? Why did this have to happen just when she was trying to negotiate an important business deal, not to mention trying to attract Sebastian's attention by looking cool and sophisticated? Should she maintain a blasé facade and casually mention the incident? Or was it all right to panic as long as she didn't become hysterical? What would Erin do?

Megan sat perfectly still, wracked by indecision.

Maybe if she could find the contact lens quickly, before Sebastian returned to her side, she could retrieve it without mishap. It had to be somewhere on or near the couch. She was running her hand over the cushion next to her legs when he returned with her wineglass. She froze.

He held it out to her. "I must admit your offer intrigues me," he said.

With only one lens in her eye, Megan found she had no depth perception. She reached tentatively for the glass, not wanting to interrupt Sebastian with an explanation of her predicament in case he was about to accept her deal.

Sitting down, he reached for another sandwich and gestured for her to help herself. "Your offer has some definite possibilities, Megan." He took a bite and chewed slowly, then studied the sandwich critically. "You should try the egg salad sandwiches. They're good." He paused, then added pensively, "I wonder what the caterers put in them? I just bit into something salty and crunchy."

Megan felt the blood drain from her face. "Crunchy?" she repeated weakly. "Before you say anything else, there's something I've got to tell you."

"Now, you're not going to amend your business proposition, are you?" Sebastian teased. "I'm really very interested in it."

Megan's mouth went dry. She shook her head and took a long swallow of wine. What could she say? "I'm sorry, but I think you've just eaten my contact lens?" Or something less direct, like: "I seem to be experiencing a medical emergency, and I'd appreciate it if you'd call me a cab?" She agonized, searching for the right remark, feeling slightly sick as she watched Sebastian consume the rest of his sandwich. She drained her wine in a single gulp. If she told him, would he get so angry that their negotiations would come to an abrupt halt? She couldn't take that chance.

"You drank your wine in such a hurry!" he remarked with surprise. "Is something wrong?"

"Wrong?" Did her voice sound as shrill to him as it did to her? "No, not at all."

"I'll tell you what I'd like to do, Megan. Tomorrow I'll stop by your store and take a look at your books. If everything's satisfactory, there's no reason why we can't do business together."

She stood up on rubbery legs, wondering how she was going to drive across San Francisco with only one eye in working order. But she hadn't taken more than three steps when Sebastian placed a hand on her shoulder. "Wait, Megan. Aren't you forgetting something?"

She turned to look at him, trying to focus on his face.

A roguish grin spread over his features. Opening a palm, he held out her contact lens. "I found this on the sofa cushion. Is it yours by any chance?"

CHAPTER TWO

"DO YOU HAVE any idea how I felt?" Megan threw the pencil down on the desk and leaned back to survey her shop, now devoid of customers. She wearily rubbed the back of her neck. "I wanted to look him square in the face with my one good eye, deny I'd ever seen that contact lens, and walk out the door without as much as a backward glance."

"That bit of bravado would have cost you dearly," Erin observed. "Contact lenses are far from cheap."

"I know," Megan admitted. "That's why I smiled like an idiot, mumbled something incoherent, and practically ran to his downstairs bathroom. When I came out, he was talking to the caterers. I got my things and slipped out when he wasn't looking. After living through that incident, I decided I had met my quota of humiliation for the month."

Erin picked up the pot of freshly brewed coffee, poured some into her own cup, and filled Megan's favorite Chip and Dale mug. It was after store hours, and the two women were enjoying a short break before officially closing up shop.

Erin returned to her seat and ran another long column of figures through the adding machine. "Megan, this account simply doesn't balance. I've gone over it again and again."

Megan closed the accounts-payable ledger and set it aside. "Oh, damn," she muttered softly. "I've got to get these books in order. After last night I'm not sure if Sebastian's still planning to stop by, but if he does, I'd better be able to convince him I'm an efficient businesswoman. Otherwise I don't stand a chance of getting him to agree to my alternative to his rent increase."

She stared pensively at her coffee. She'd come so far in the past year and a half! Surely fate wouldn't be so cruel as to take everything she had worked so hard for away from her. It wasn't as if she hadn't paid her dues.

Losing her parents at such a young age and being sent to live with her aunt had been very difficult for her. She'd had to fight for every scrap of independence she'd achieved. Marrying Jim Lord, a man fourteen years her senior, had seemed her ticket to freedom. Even Aunt Beatrice had approved, saying that a practical, mature man with a no-nonsense approach to life was just what Megan needed.

Aunt Beatrice had certainly helped make the marriage possible: Jim was almost the only man she had let Megan date. Aunt Beatrice was sure that his influence would dispel her niece's silly romantic fantasies once and for all.

Megan had loved Jim. At least she had thought so at the time. Now, looking back, she realized that her love for Jim had probably been her biggest fantasy. He had been the knight in shining armor who was going to take her away to his romantic castle and shower her with love. As it had turned out, her image of him had proven to be quite different from the real man.

Her youth had been partly to blame for the failure of the marriage. She had married right out of high school. By the time she was twenty-four, she had realized she was trapped in a loveless relationship. Jim sincerely cared for her, as much as he was able to care, but what he wanted most was a woman to clean his home and oversee his two teenage sons while he was busy farming. Yet the boys, who were more like brothers to Megan than sons, never seemed to pay much attention to her.

It seemed that love, the idyllic kind of love she had dreamed about as a teenager, simply didn't exist. At least not for her. Though she liked and respected Jim, she gradually came to realize that she would never feel more than friendship for him. She had no business being married to him.

A few days after Jim's oldest son graduated from high school, she'd finally accepted the fact that, unless she made some changes in her life, she'd never find the fulfillment she sought. It took her another long year to gather her courage and ask for a divorce.

Trying to contend with the feeling that life had cheated her, trying to believe in herself, despite the warnings of Jim and her aunt that she would fail miserably if she tried to make it on her own—these struggles now formed a jumble of painful images in her mind.

Still, she had made it. She was here in San Francisco, and at twenty-six she owned her own shop. The drive to succeed on her own, after all else had failed her, had kept her going. If she could only manage to hold onto her dream . . .

"You know," she said slowly to Erin, "I really wasn't kidding when I said I can't afford to pay the rent increase."

"I've already offered to help," her friend said quietly.

"No." Megan was adamant. "When I was trying to open the store, I found that, even with my savings and divorce settlement, I needed one thousand dollars more than I had. You loaned me the difference. That was enough."

"But I didn't do it just for you," Erin protested. "I wanted to invest my money in something I felt had solid potential."

"I appreciate the vote of confidence." Megan smiled warmly. "If I'd doubted my ability to make it in this business, I'd never have accepted the money."

"I know. That's what made you such a good risk as far as I was concerned." Erin stood up and stretched. "So it's in my best interest to help you out at the store. The sooner you reach your goal, the faster I'll get paid back."

"And I presume the fact that we're friends has no bearing on the matter, right?" Megan teased.

"Well . . ." Erin shrugged. "I didn't say that exactly." Their eyes met, and they started to laugh. "Megan, do you realize how much you've changed since I first met you? You were working in the lingerie department at Newman's department store. I asked you to help me find a black lace teddy in my size, and you reached up to the top shelf and accidentally knocked all the clothes down on yourself. You were covered with black lace underwear! Suddenly a really cute guy walked by and whistled. You looked like you might pass out from embarrassment."

"It never would have happened if you'd just bought the day-of-the-week panties as I suggested," Megan said. "I still remember finding your wallet on the floor next to the counter later that day, with everything in it except your telephone number. I figured you'd dropped it when you helped me pick up the underwear. I felt so guilty. When I checked the address on your driver's license, I discovered it was on the way to my rooming house. I convinced the manager to let me take it to you, saying it would be good for customer relations." Megan adopted a conspiratorial whisper. "It took a lot of courage on my part, you know. My aunt had told me what type of girl bought *that* kind of underwear."

Erin laughed loudly. "I'm glad you came by that night. I was trying to get used to the idea that I'd have to start looking for another place to live. The rent was too high for me to handle without a roommate. Although my scholarship had paid for my tuition, I still had lots of expenses. Then, all of a sudden, there you were! It must have been fate."

"Either that or someone up there decided we'd be perfect roommates. I'd be a good influence on you—"

"While I taught you to have fun and not worry so much about everything," Erin finished. She picked up her purse from the floor and headed for the door. "I better be going. It's almost five o'clock, and I'm working graveyard at the radio station tonight. The disc jockeys will fall apart unless their favorite engineer is in the control room, pushing all the right switches." She reached for her raincoat.

"Megan, do you realize it's been almost a year since we sat at the table imagining the sorts of bizarre merchandise a store could sell? You came up with so many funny ideas that I knew you'd be successful if you opened your own novelty shop. Aren't you glad I talked you into taking a chance and starting your own business?"

"I don't know," Megan said, only half teasing. "Ask me a year from now."

Erin searched her handbag for her keys. "By the way,

if you can wait until tomorrow, I'll help you figure out why those ledgers don't balance."

"Thanks, but one way or another I'm finishing the bookkeeping tonight. I've been lucky so far that Sebastian hasn't stopped by, but I intend to be ready for him. If he doesn't come to see me, I'll make it a point to find him. I've got to get this matter settled soon."

"Try not to work all night, will you? Everyone's entitled to a rest." Erin regarded Megan squarely. "I worry about you. You work too hard. You really should try and get out more. Do something you enjoy, and get away from the store for a change."

"Stop fussing over me. I like my work."

Erin shrugged. "I give up."

Standing outside the store, Megan watched her friend go down the stairs and across the parking lot. After making sure she had reached her car safely, Megan returned to her desk and got to work. During the next hour she scarcely looked up. Finally, no closer to unearthing the mistake in the books than when she had started, she crossed the room to the farthest corner. Folding her arms over her chest, she leaned against the wall and aimed a murderous look at the columnar sheets strewn across her desk. Maybe she should think of a way to cover the mistake in case Sebastian dropped in unexpectedly before she had figured out the problem. The last thing she needed was for him to discover she had made a minor blunder in the bookkeeping.

Minor blunder. As she mulled over the words, a smile crept over her face. There was an answer, after all! She'd simply start an extra account for Minah B. Lunder. For the month of July, for instance, she was five dollars over, so she would credit Minah B. Lunder with five dollars. August showed a deficit of fifteen dollars and ten cents, so Minah B. Lunder's account, already credited with five dollars, would show that he needed to pay that additional amount.

Megan finished up thirty minutes later. What a cinch! Not that she planned to leave the books that way forever. But until she really had time to sift through all the figures, her solution would give Sebastian a general overview of how her store was doing. It wasn't as if she was *cheating* anyone. She had *not* changed any of the amounts. They were all there, showing a deficit or a surplus in accordance with what her figures indicated.

Swinging one leg over the arm of her chair, she leaned back and relaxed, her thoughts drifting to Sebastian. Remembering the details of their first meeting with a grimace, she began to imagine a quite different encounter. She envisioned herself sitting next to Sebastian on the sofa in his den, looking simply stunning in a silver sequined gown. Taking the wineglass slowly from his hand, she leaned over and boldly kissed his firm mouth. His response was swift and fiery, then gentle and deeply passionate. The unhurried pace of her seduction made the flames of desire burn more fiercely between them. At last, pushing him gently away, she suggested he remove his clothes. She could see him standing before her as he discarded each piece, until his naked body was exposed to her gaze. Taking his hand, she led him back to the sofa and coaxed him into a reclining position, his back against the cushions. With teasing kisses and tantalizing caresses she provoked and taunted him, burning away the last vestiges of his control in a frenzy of desire. Engulfed in the searing white heat of passion, he cried out her name. She clung to him, knowing he was hers, basking in the sweetness of their love.

Megan shook her head and laughed. If all that had really begun to happen, she'd never have lived through it! Her courage would have faltered, and she'd have died of a heart attack the moment he began to remove his pants.

Was she destined to feel inadequate around Sebastian? She hoped not. Yet there was no denying that he was far out of her realm of experience. Jim Lord had hardly been a hunk!

Remembering the way Sebastian's eyes had held hers, she felt a shiver run up her spine. She had seen desire there, as well as the promise of a sensuality that far transcended anything she had known before. She stood up angrily, suddenly restless. She really was hopeless!

The wonderfully vivid romantic imagination that had led her aunt to classify her as an impractical daydreamer was working overtime once again. Megan could still remember the time she was fifteen and fell in love with a popular actor after seeing him on a poster. For weeks she had faithfully written him anonymous love letters, hoping against hope that he'd somehow discover her identity and carry her off to his glamorous Hollywood world. Her bubble had burst when she'd read that he'd married his high school sweetheart.

And then there was the time she'd decided the new history teacher was really a secret agent. She *had* seen him sneaking around town looking guilty. But when Megan had disclosed her suspicions, her aunt had laughed at her. It had turned out that the man didn't want any of his students or their parents to find out he was dating the chorus director!

Now, without knowing much at all about Sebastian Gladstone, Megan was mentally filling in all the blanks. And, just as she had as a youngster, she was becoming more and more infatuated with the product of her fantasies.

Her romantic imagination had frequently caused her problems. She shook her head in silent disapproval. She had only been on a few dates since arriving in San Francisco, but even then she had managed to fantasize the guys all out of proportion. Invariably, the men had failed to live up to her wild expectations, and she'd ended up being disappointed. Surely she wouldn't go through the rest of her life repeating the same mistake over and over again! Her disastrous marriage to Jim should have been lesson enough.

She stopped pacing and returned to her chair. Wouldn't she ever learn? The only thing she really knew about Sebastian was that he was a very handsome man . . . with blue eyes one could drown in, a torso so solid and perfectly structured he would rival any of Hollywood's leading men, and a narrow waist and slim hips that would have teased any woman's senses.

Suddenly a deep male voice sounded behind her. "Hello."

Startled, Megan jumped and spun around in her chair so quickly that she almost fell off. "What . . ."

Dangling a set of keys in his hand, Sebastian stood just inside her office doorway. Wearing a powder-blue cashmere pullover and tan wool slacks, he had the classic look of a businessman who'd just come off the golf course.

"I can understand why you look surprised, Megan, but why in the world are you blushing?" he asked, his eyes shining with roguish merriment, his smile dazzling her.

"It must be the light." She turned away and made a show of straightening her desk. Coming unexpectedly face to face with the very man who had featured so prominently in her fantasies just moments before was proving decidedly unnerving. It would be enough to throw any sane person into confusion, she concluded. With effort, she regained control of herself. "Would you like to see my books?" she asked politely.

He laughed. "I'll take a look at whatever you're willing to show me." Something about the way his eyes twinkled made her suspect he had somehow guessed what she'd been thinking.

She tried to swallow the lump that had suddenly lodged

in her throat. It wouldn't be smart to let him think she was easily unsettled. "I'm sure I don't know what else you could possibly be interested in seeing," she said primly.

"Don't you, Megan?" he asked in a tone that implied a lot more than he'd said. He raised one eyebrow provocatively. "Don't you ever . . . imagine things that are hidden? Or mentally act out emotions you would never actually express?"

Damn him! It was as if he could reach her mind! She started to clear off her desk to make room for the large accounting ledgers stacked on top of each other on the floor, then abruptly stopped what she was doing. "Wait a minute." She stared at him. "How in the world did you get in here? I locked that door after Erin left." ·

"I was wondering when you'd get around to asking that. You might have locked the door from the inside, but you were kind enough to leave these"—he held out her keys—"on the outside."

With a sharp intake of breath, she opened the top drawer of her desk, where she usually kept the keys. They weren't there. She groaned. "So much for security."

"How long have these been there?" he asked. "Do you realize anyone could have come in?"

She nodded miserably. "I must have left them there after lunch, when Erin picked up some merchandise for me. I propped the door open while we brought things in from the car. Afterward I got so busy putting everything away, I guess I forgot all about the keys."

Megan cringed inwardly. By now Sebastian must have decided she was an ideal candidate for a brain transplant. Maybe a direct approach would help. She cleared her throat and faced him squarely. "I want to be honest with you. I've really been trying, or should I say *hoping*, to impress you, but I'm not doing a very good job of it."

"On the contrary, you've done an excellent job," he said, making himself comfortable on a tall wooden stool. "I'm sold on you. In fact, if you say the word, I'll be happy to take you home with me."

Megan grimaced. "Please, I'm trying to be serious."

"So am I."

"You can't be!"

He laughed and gestured for her to continue. "I'm listening."

"A year and a half ago I arrived in San Francisco without the faintest idea of where I'd live or how I'd support myself. Everything I owned was in the two suitcases I'd brought with me. I worked for ten months in a department store, then spent four months getting Off the Beaten Path ready for business. This place is all that matters to me now. It may not look like much to you, but to me it represents the culmination of a dream that seemed all but hopeless when I first left Missouri. I've worked very hard for all of this, and I'm extremely proud of it.

"But my store has only been open four months," she explained, "and although my business has increased steadily, I'm still operating on a shoestring budget. I can't afford to hire any help, so that means I have to do everything. I'm a bookkeeper, a saleslady, a store manager, a buyer, and a cleaning woman. Sometimes I get so busy that not all the jobs get done to perfection, but they *do* get done."

He sat perfectly still, his gaze steady on her. There was a calmness about him, a quiet inner strength. His expression was openly speculative, but for an instant Megan thought she saw a glimmer of approval in the depths of his eyes.

Encouraged, she went on. "On top of everything else, I've been under a lot of pressure since I heard about the possibility of a rent increase. I knew I couldn't afford to pay it, but by the same token, I wanted my shop to stay right where it is. The only way I could do that was to negotiate an alternate deal with you."

She cleared her throat. "The reason I'm taking the time to explain all this is because I want you to realize that, although you may think I'm careless and scatter-brained, I'm neither. I couldn't have put all the pieces together and made this store a reality if that were the case. I've offered you a sound business proposition, one that will benefit both of us."

Sebastian clasped her hand warmly. "I realized that from the beginning, Megan. You've come up with an innovative proposal that seems quite reasonable. Relax. Everything will work out fine."

Megan's spirits rose at his words—then sank back down to her toes as he picked up her ledger and began to leaf through it. Feigning confidence, she said, "Like I said, feel free to check my financial progress. You'll find that I've come a long way in a very short time. If you accept my terms, you can be sure I'll work very hard to make certain your percentage is a profitable one. I'll do everything in my power to answer any questions you might have, any time you have them. Every facet of my business isn't perfect, but I'll make sure this store is a sound business investment."

"From what I see here," he said slowly, "you really can't afford to pay anyone two percent of your net profit. If these accounts are accurate, you're barely breaking even."

"That's true, but look at the progression. My net has gone up at least seven percent each month. And I have lots more good ideas, which I intend to begin investi-gating soon."

"Like what?"

She took note of his light-blue pullover and conservative white shirt collar. An expensive gold watch circled his masculine wrist. He certainly had the look of old money about him. Was he ready for her ideas? Or would he consider her business too marginal to be worth his time?

"Have you worked out your ideas yet?" he asked when she didn't answer.

She nodded slowly. If he was going to invest in her store, he might as well get used to the fact that Off the Beaten Path was far from ordinary.

"About a month ago one of my customers came in on a rainy day holding a soaking wet poodle. She kept complaining about how she hated to take Snookums for a walk when it was raining. After she left, I thought about her problem. People are always concerned about their pets. Umbrellas are great for people, but how do you shield an animal that's walking several feet away from you? Then I got a wonderful idea for what I'm going to market as a London Dogg. It's a khaki trench-coat-style raincoat for pooches, but the belt around the dog's middle holds an umbrella. We'll keep the umbrella extremely lightweight by using a very short nylon pole. The plastic canopy will give the dog maximum protection by opening just over the animal's head.

"I'm also planning to develop monogrammed pet sweaters and collars," she went on. "I've received permission to be the West Coast outlet for Designer Dogwear, items carrying the insignia of famous dogs and cats like Lassie and Sylvester."

Sebastian's expression had grown more and more astonished. Finally he collapsed into loud laughter. "I hate to ask, but how do you get an animal to let you put these fashions on him?"

"Dogs can be trained," Megan explained seriously, ignoring his amusement. "Look how they're taught to carry packs during wartime, or to pull sleds in the arctic. Take the London Doggs, for example. Once the owners see the advantages of returning home with dry doggies, they'll work on training their pets. The benefits far outweigh the problems." Megan rushed on, filled with excitement. "I spoke to a lady just a few weeks ago who came in selling homemade pet products. She said she'd be glad to sew the London Doggs for me. We'll offer small, medium, and large sizes. Don't you think it's a fantastic concept?"

Sebastian opened his mouth to answer her, then closed it again, shaking his head. "Tell me about your other ideas."

"Well," she said enthusiastically, "I got another idea when I went to an art exhibit with Erin. Wouldn't it be neat to appear in a historical photograph or painting? For example, think of seeing your own face in the boat with Washington as he's crossing the Delaware. Or perhaps as one of the Marines raising the flag on Iwo Jima. I contacted an artist's studio a block from here. With the props the local theater promised us in exchange for a small rental fee, we'll be able to provide this extra service for our customers."

Sebastian's eyes gleamed with a gentle warmth that made Megan's toes tingle. "You seem to be a whirlwind of creativity," he observed.

His tone puzzled her. Was he trying to tell her in a polite way she was crazy? "Since you obviously have doubts," she said, "I'll guarantee that in the event Off the Beaten Path goes out of business before my lease expires, any remaining cash from my liquidated inventory will be yours. Also, you may consider me out of business if I'm ever unable to pay my next month's rent in advance."

Sebastian gave her a skeptical look. "You'd still have

debts to settle with the companies from which you've received merchandise. Are you sure you'd have enough money left over after that to pay me?"

She looked away, inhaling deeply. This talk of bankruptcy was giving her a headache. "Most of the inventory you see here has already been paid for," she explained. "Dealing with my suppliers little by little on a cash basis enables me to get some very good discounts on wholesale prices. I also have a diamond pendant I inherited from my mother. It's been in the family for years. The diamonds are what they call old-mine cut, so they're not worth as much as diamonds that have the brilliant cut with fifty-six facets. Still, the brooch is set in platinum, and when I had it appraised a year ago, it was worth fifty-four hundred dollars. I'll turn it over to you as collateral, along with the written appraisal Enchanted Jewelers made for me. Will that be sufficient?"

He hesitated. "Go ahead and keep the pin, but do give me a copy of the appraisal. I'll have my attorneys draw up a contract. When they finish, I'll drop it by for you to look over. Something tells me that doing business with you is going to be quite an experience," he added dryly. "We might *even* make some money."

"I'll do everything in my power to see that your investment remains a sound one," she promised, extending her hand for him to shake.

But instead of shaking it, he cupped it between both of his hands. His touch was firm and warm, and it evoked a responding thrill in her that threatened to unnerve her. "Megan, your optimism and resourcefulness are refreshing qualities in the tough and often cynical business world," he said. "Your enthusiasm may rub off on me yet. I've never met anyone quite like you."

The heat of his palms seemed to sear into her very bones, making her heart beat wildly. She sought frantically for something witty to say, but the sensations he was arousing wiped all but the simplest thoughts from her mind.

Feeling terribly awkward, she finally found a safe subject. "Well, Sebastian, now that we're business partners, why don't you pour us a cup of coffee while I finish putting these things away?" She grabbed a box of greeting cards and gave a little wave to hurry him into action.

Picking up on her buoyant mood, Sebastian bowed deeply and replied, "As you wish, madam." He poured their cups and brought them to the counter near the ledgers. "Do you require anything else, madam?"

"No, Sebastian, that will be all," she answered primly. With a curt nod he made himself comfortable in the chair and began leafing through the top ledger.

Megan scrambled up her small stepladder and stretched to reach the high shelf where the stationery was stored. As she reached the top rung, the ladder began to wobble. She grabbed the shelf with her free hand, struggling to keep her balance. "Actually, there *is* something else, please," she called. "Would you steady the ladder while I climb down? There's no room for a broken leg in my deficit column."

Sebastian looked up, realized her predicament, and muttered an oath. "Why didn't you ask for help?" Placing one foot on a lower step and his hands on her waist, he guided her gently down until her feet touched the floor.

On firm ground once again, she looked up into his eyes, intending to thank him, but the emotion she saw there stole the words from her mouth. There was no mistaking the smoldering passion that burned in his blue gaze.

Their eyes held as Sebastian pulled her slowly against his hard length, molding her to his rigid thighs, his hands spanning her narrow waist and moving restlessly up and down her spine. She sensed a controlled urgency in his movements that sent a golden ache spreading through her. She parted her lips willingly as his mouth descended to hers. His kiss was gentle, and confident in its power to persuade.

She melted against him, trembling with a passion that left her pliable in his arms and vulnerable to his silent demands. Her senses were reeling. She had never before experienced such powerful need. He deepened the kiss, and she was lost in sweet, swirling sensations. At last he raised his head and gazed tenderly down at her.

"I haven't been able to get you out of my mind for even a moment," he murmured. "I keep remembering the way your clothes clung to your body when you emerged from the pool. You looked so small, so vulnerable, so beautiful. The thought of you has been driving me crazy."

She drew back from him, trying to clear her thoughts. Had she gone completely mad? This man was her landlord, her business partner! How could she let him kiss her? How could she risk leading him to believe that she was part of the deal they had just negotiated?

The thought frightened her into action. Stepping out of the circle of his arms, she crossed the room and turned to face him.

For a brief moment, as she saw the look of raw desire on his features, she fought an impulse to run back into his arms. She broke the spell by looking away, swallowed, and gathered her courage. "I'm not a fringe benefit included in our agreement, Sebastian. My business is one thing, my personal life quite another."

"I know that." He regarded her quizzically. "Have I frightened you? That wasn't my intention. Megan, you're the most desirable woman I've ever met. You're sensual and beautiful, yet you seem scarcely aware of it."

Her heart soared. But she was too embarrassed to know how to respond. "I, uh . . . I think you're making far too much of me, Sebastian."

"I don't agree. But I won't argue the point. Let's go out for a drink and celebrate our conclusion of a mutually profitable business deal. I'll take you to my favorite haunt. What do you say?"

Surely she couldn't turn him down now. If she did, he'd think she *was* afraid of him. Besides, it was hardly good business practice to refuse to have a drink with the man who was, in effect, her store's newest investor. Her decision made, she reached for her coat. "Where are you taking us?"

"To the west side of the city. You won't believe the view of the Pacific this place has."

Sebastian locked the door behind them and activated the alarm each tenant was required to use. "My car's right over there." He pointed to a small red Porsche parked under a streetlight.

"Nice."

"Where's yours?"

She pointed to a battered old sedan parked near the door. "Meet Wally."

"Wally?"

"Wally, the wonder car. Erin says it's a wonder he's still running."

Sebastian laughed. "You're going to need it to drive to work tomorrow, so why don't I follow you home and take you from there?"

"Good idea."

Less than fifteen minutes from the shopping center lay Megan's neighborhood, a cluster of picturesque but tired-looking Victorian residences that had been converted from single-family homes to smaller apartments. In the dim light of the street lamps, the buildings looked like gingerbread houses from a children's book of fairy tales.

Parking in front of Megan's apartment house wasn't difficult since only four tenants currently occupied the weather-stained pink and white gabled home, and two of the women shared one car. The neighborhood wasn't the greatest, but when Megan's shop began to make more money, she planned to find a nicer place.

She slammed her car door shut and looked up at the second-story window facing the street. "That's ours," she told Sebastian, pointing. Recalling how beautiful his home was, she felt a little embarrassed. "Erin and I share a one-bedroom apartment. It's a little cramped," she said sheepishly, "but since our work hours don't coincide, we're usually not home at the same time. It saves us from tripping over each other."

She debated whether or not to ask Sebastian upstairs, then decided that probably wasn't a good idea. "I'm ready to go whenever you are," she said brightly.

He opened the passenger door and made a sweeping gesture. "My chariot awaits."

Megan hopped in and buckled her seat belt while he sprinted around to the driver's side. With a roar of the engine and a shifting of gears, they were off, speeding up and down a virtual roller coaster of steep streets. Megan noticed that Sebastian seemed to take particular pleasure in accelerating the small sports car as they climbed, then easing off the gas as they catapulted over the top and dove downward.

Her stomach rose and fell correspondingly. "You seem to be enjoying this," she observed wryly.

He laughed. "Actually, yes. It's even more fun than an amusement-park ride because I'm in control. It's a combination of riding the roller coaster and racing cars. Not bad, huh?"

"Whatever turns you on."

"Oh? That sounds like an invitation I'll be eager to pursue as soon as I've got my hands free."

She shifted restlessly in her seat. "Only if I've got my track shoes on," she retorted. Was he flirting with her because he liked her, or did he do it automatically with every woman he met? As they drove past Sutro Heights Park, she turned to look at him. "Are you going out the Great Highway?"

He nodded. "There's a restaurant called Seal Rock Mansion out this way. It's set on a high cliff and rather isolated, but that gives it wonderful atmosphere. At low tide there's a stretch of beach below the cliffs. If you've got comfortable shoes on, we can go for a walk."

She gave her low-heeled espadrilles a cursory glance. "A little sand won't hurt these at all."

After parking along the highway behind a long row of cars, Sebastian led Megan inside. The foyer opened onto a large area filled with linen-topped tables, all with a view of the shoreline. Prints of old sailing vessels hung on the walls.

Several of the waiters and customers recognized Sebastian, who waved in greeting and stopped to chat briefly with the bartender before sitting down at a table across from Megan. "What would you like to drink?" he asked.

"How good are the piña coladas here?"

"Excellent, I'm told, but I hope you don't mind if I order a scotch for myself. I don't care much for mixed drinks."

"I wouldn't dream of forcing a piña colada on anyone," she replied good-naturedly.

Their drinks arrived from the bar quickly. "Jerry," Sebastian told their waiter, "we'll bring the glasses back, all right?"

"Going for a walk along the beach?" he asked. "You just missed a beautiful sunset."

Sebastian shrugged and led Megan through heavy doors and down a flight of steps outside. The ocean was dotted with giant rocks near the shoreline. The waves glimmered in the soft glow of an ascending full moon. "I usually like to find a comfortable spot, sit on the sand, and watch the waves come rolling in," Sebastian said. "Does that sound okay with you?"

She nodded and fell into step beside him, questions racing through her mind. What was it about him that made her feel so restless? The very foundations of her life seemed to be threatened. She was an adult and no longer believed in love at first sight. But she was at a loss to define this feeling, which seemed to transcend the purely physical. She wanted to know Sebastian thoroughly, to find out everything about him.

She sipped her creamy, cirtrusy drink, finding its coolness a pleasant contrast to the warmth that seemed to be spreading through her. She shook her head, fighting against the spine-tingling sensations.

"All right," Sebastian replied, mistaking her gesture, "we can walk if you prefer."

She glanced up abruptly and began to laugh. "This is crazy."

"What? Walking along the beach?" He cocked his head. "It's actually a common pastime in California."

She raised her chin, suddenly feeling carefree and adventurous. "I'll tell you what I'd really like to do." She eased down on her knees and sat back on her heels.

"What?" he asked, clearly puzzled.

"I want to build a sand castle." She secured her glass beside her by burying the base in the sand. "How about right here?"

He stood looking perplexed as she shifted to a sitting position with her legs to one side, digging in the sand with her hands. "You're kidding!" he exclaimed. "I haven't met a girl who wanted to build sand castles since the first grade. I hope you don't expect me to grovel in the sand, too."

She glanced up at him. "Come on. You had your fun driving the car. Now it's my turn."

Chuckling, he squatted down beside her. "You are the most unusual woman I've ever met. I can't figure you out at all."

"Why's that?" she asked, shaping a pile of sand to form the castle's foundation.

"Earlier tonight you were a determined business-woman. Now, I'm dealing with a bright-eyed youngster who seems half a beat behind the tempo of the big city. I don't know what to make of you, Megan Lord. You're like a breath of fresh air."

"Maybe I'm a mixture of everything you've noticed, and a few more qualities and contradictions you've yet to see."

He sat back on his heels and sipped his drink as she continued to shape the sand. She was grateful for the activity because suddenly the desire to reach out and touch him was almost overwhelming. As long as she kept busy, maybe she could resist the temptation. "Everyone has different sides of his or her personality," she went on. "You, for instance, are quite complex yourself."

"What do you mean by that?" he asked, laughing.

Should she tell him how confident he always appeared to her, how intimidating he sometimes seemed, yet how she found herself responding to the warm sensitivity in his blue eyes? "You always seem to be in command of the situation," she finally managed.

"Is that what you find intimidating?" he challenged gently.

Caught off guard by his uncanny perception, she lost her concentration, and her hand smashed through the sand tower she'd been forming. She recovered quickly and continued as if nothing unusual had happened. "You don't intimidate me at all," she denied. "Oh, I admit I was a little apprehensive about doing business with you, since there was a lot at stake for me, but that's just natural."

"I've already agreed to your terms. Why are you still nervous?"

She panicked briefly. What could she say? Certainly not that he had become the star of her most recent, and most erotic, fantasies. Nor that her attraction for him was growing exponentially with each encounter.

She was waging a war within herself, torn between the romantic side of her nature that urged her to allow her emotions free rein, and the pragmatic side that demanded she acknowledge the danger of doing so. Every rational thought warned her to fight her feelings, to avoid getting involved at all costs. Yet, the strength of her need drew her in a very different direction.

"I think you're misreading me, Sebastian," she said, hoping to lead the conversation away from herself. "It's not nervousness you see, but curiosity. I want to know more about you, but I'm not very patient. I want to get past the initial awkwardness that always exists between two people when they first meet. I want to go on to a more comfortable stage of friendship."

Had she inadvertently revealed too much about herself? Perhaps it would have been wiser to play the games Erin assured her were guaranteed to heighten a man's interest. Being mysterious and aloof was probably a better way to keep him interested.

"Ask anything you want to know about me," Sebastian said.

She was reassured by his direct approach, which indicated he was a man in touch with his own strengths and weaknesses, one who had learned to know and accept exactly who he was. She asked the question that had been in her mind from the beginning. "Is it true you refused to go into your family's business?"

"Yes. My father and I had been at odds for years. He never allowed me to run the business the way I wanted to. I felt that if I was supposed to shoulder the responsibility, he should give me full control. But he refused to grant me any autonomy whatsoever. Rather than stay and accept a situation I felt would hurt both of us, I decided to go out on my own."

"Do you miss your family?"

"We didn't part as enemies. My father simply gave me a small share of the estate, told me that was all I'd ever get from him, and wished me luck." He shook his head sadly. "The press made it sound as if I had inherited enough money to start my own Treasury Department, but that's far from the truth. Had I stayed home, I would have, but by becoming independent, I've had to work hard for whatever I've achieved." He paused and met her eyes. "Much like you."

With seeming effort, he broke their gaze. "Since my divorce two years ago, I've dated a lot of women," he went on, "but I've been committed to none of them. I've gone to parties, the theater, and whatever else came along. I had no desire to change that until I met you. Now all of a sudden that kind of life seems empty and pointless to me."

At his tentative smile, so full of masculine charm, she found her pulse racing out of control. He was devastating! How she wished he would kiss her again . . . She couldn't help but smile back at him.

Had she lost her mind? He was bound to think she was encouraging him! How did he know so exactly what to say to get the responses he wanted from her? He was more dangerous than she had even suspected. Her curiosity, however, refused to yield to caution. "What happened to end your marriage?" she asked softly.

His eyes clouded with anger . . . or was it pain? She

couldn't be sure. "I had known Ann all my life. Our families were friends even before we were born. But it wasn't until I graduated from college that I fell in love with her. Everyone thought we were a perfect match." He paused and downed the rest of his scotch in one large swallow.

"Our marriage lasted for three years. I was busy working with my father, and she was always shopping or involved with activities at our club. I suppose she simply didn't notice what was happening between my father and I. Or maybe she didn't care as long as she got what she wanted. I don't know. When I told her I was leaving to start my own business, she refused to come with me. She was spoiled, selfish. She knew my announcement meant there would be rough times ahead, that we'd have to alter our lifestyle considerably. She wasn't willing to do that. I realized then that she loved playing the role of a rich man's wife more than she loved me. That hurt. Plus knowing that I had spent the last three years of my life living a lie. It takes more to make a marriage than a sheet of paper."

"I'm sorry," Megan murmured, aching at the pain she saw in his eyes. Without thinking, she reached for his hand and held it tenderly between her own. "I didn't mean to open up an old wound. Forgive me."

His expression was kind, understanding. "There's nothing to forgive, sweetheart."

His words catapulted Megan into a world that moved in slow motion. He entwined his fingers in her hair, coaxing her head backward and tilting it toward his descending lips.

His lips barely touched hers at first. They tasted lightly and lingered in a slow, moist caress. He tantalized her, moving his mouth languidly over hers, until it flowered open, and his tongue became a devilish instrument that left her gasping, feeling as if she were being enveloped in a blazing fire. Freeing his hand from hers, he sought the fullness of her breast and cupped it gently in his palm.

A sweet weakness seized her. She pressed herself against his hand, wanting to increase the intimacy between them, oblivious to anything save the desire to be immersed in the liquid fire of his caress. The intensity of her response left her stunned and confused. She wanted him. No man had ever made her want him like this.

Her fevered brain demanded that she tell him to stop, but the words were trapped at the back of her throat. Then, abruptly, the sound of voices coming closer broke the spell, and she pushed away.

"Don't be afraid, Megan. Trust me," he murmured close to her ear. "I won't let our relationship hurt you in any way." His eyes seemed to peer into her soul. "Don't try to fight what's happening. If it's our destiny to become lovers, nothing you can do will stop it."

The words jolted her out of her sensual haze. It was happening all over again. As soon as she allowed a man into her life, he started making decisions for her. She moved farther away from him. "Thank you, Sebastian, but I don't need your advice. I have no intention of letting you make love to me." She stood up and brushed the sand from her clothing. "As I told you before, I'm not part of the deal we negotiated. You and I will never be lovers."

"Is that a challenge?" He stood up, too, and faced her, the trace of a smile on his lips.

"No, it's not a challenge," she said more forcefully. "As far as you're concerned, Sebastian, it's a simple fact."

CHAPTER THREE

MEGAN STORMED AROUND the kitchen, trying to sort out her thoughts. She stuffed the last English muffin into the toaster and forced herself to concentrate on the magazine article open in front of her.

Minutes passed. The acrid scent of something burning made her wrinkle her nose and look up. With a gasp, she jumped up, turning over her chair in her haste, and pulled the cord of the toaster from the wall socket. She made a face. She had just incinerated her breakfast.

A lingering puff of smoke curled upward in wispy gray tendrils. Grabbing the toaster with oven mitts, she turned the defunct appliance upside down and shook charred muffin slices loose, letting them fall with a thud into the wastebasket. Her day was off to a terrible start.

At the sound of a key turning in the lock, she glanced

up. "Erin! How was work last night?" she asked with forced good humor.

Her roommate sniffed the air cautiously. "First, tell me about the fire."

Megan scowled. "No fire. I simply cremated the only English muffin we had left."

Erin removed her coat and tossed it on top of their faded gold and brown striped couch. "Is there anything else to eat?"

Megan put down her magazine. "I'll look."

Erin slumped into the yellow vinyl chair across from where Megan had been sitting at the cluttered breakfast bar and cleared a small space for herself. "One of these days we're going to have to break down and clean this place."

The breakfast bar served a variety of purposes: as a desk, an ironing board, and as a worktable for the five-hundred-piece puzzle of a naked man that Erin had brought home for Megan. "When are you going to start working on the interesting parts of your puzzle?" Erin asked casually.

Megan refused to meet her roommate's eyes. She was *not* going to admit the painful truth that she got embarrassed just picking up those particular pieces. "I was going to be generous and give you the privilege of assembling those parts yourself," she said sourly.

"Boy, you sound depressed this morning!"

"I'm a bit down in the dumps, that's all." Megan finished searching the refrigerator. "There's part of a bagel in here covered with green mold. If that doesn't appeal to you, we have what's left of a bowl of oatmeal you stuck in here, I'd say about forty years ago." She paused. "At least, I think it's oatmeal."

Erin groaned and buried her head in her arms. "For Pete's sake, stop."

"How about some coffee?"

"I'll take it." She accepted the cup Megan placed in front of her and sipped gratefully. "Now tell me what's got you in such a bad mood."

"Nothing," Megan said airily, opening her magazine again. "Absolutely nothing."

"Try again."

Megan sighed. She knew Erin wouldn't leave her alone until she'd told her. "I'll make a deal with you," she said. "You tell me how to handle my problem with Sebastian, and I'll clean out the refrigerator."

"Okay." Erin smiled cheerfully. "That's a terrific exchange. Tell me what's wrong."

"I'm really attracted to him."

Erin's light laugh filled the room. "That's a problem?"

"Erin, the only reason he's attracted to me is because I'm different. Once the newness wears off, I know he'll get tired of me."

"If you're afraid he'll hurt you, then stop seeing him."

"That's the problem. I don't want to. He makes me feel so alive! It's exciting just to be with him. What scares me is the fact that I know he wants me and I'm not the type who can have a casual relationship with a man. Maybe my views on sex predate the sexual revolution, but to me sex is something that happens between a man and a woman who care very deeply for each other. I used to think I felt that way about Jim. I'm not going to repeat my mistake and go to bed with someone I *might* be interested in. To rush into intimacy is to cheapen it."

"If that's the way you feel, then let the relationship develop more slowly."

"If I do that, I run the risk of falling in love. The situation's going to lead to trouble no matter how I look at it. If he doesn't fall in love with me, I'll be hurt. If he does fall in love with me, we'll be led down a path I'm determined to avoid. I've just begun to run my own life, and I don't want to get so serious with someone that it begins to infringe on my freedom."

"Then you have only one alternative. Keep the relationship at the level of intimacy it is now. See him as often as you like, but make sure you don't become more emotionally involved. Enjoy the chemistry between you, but leave it at that." Erin bit her lip thoughtfully. "That's quite a tall order, but as I see it, it's your only choice."

"I think you're right. I'll just have to make sure I keep control of the situation. I'll manage somehow."

"Megan, if there's one thing I've learned about you, it's that you can do whatever you set your mind to. If this is what you want, I have no doubt you'll find a way to handle it." Erin leaned back and stretched.

"You know, I'm glad I told you about my problem." Megan rested her elbows on the table, cradling her chin in her palms. "Now I know what I have to do. I'm going to try to keep things relaxed and light between us. That way there will be less pressure on both of us." She paused. "I just hope I can handle a man as smooth as Sebastian."

"If you're really that worried, I'll try to take him off your hands," Erin suggested hopefully.

"Do, and I'll flavor your coffee with cyanide," Megan threatened playfully.

"You're so ungrateful!"

Megan glanced at the tea-kettle-shaped wall clock she had picked up at a garage sale. "I'd better get going. I have a ton of paperwork to get done before the store opens this morning."

"I should wake up at around two," Erin said, "which means I can be at the shop by two-thirty. If you can wait that long, I'll watch the store while you treat yourself to a leisurely lunch."

"Thanks," Megan said, flashing her friend a grateful smile. "It's a deal."

* * *

Megan arrived at the shopping center eager to start work. Today she was determined to keep her mind off Sebastian. Thinking about him was guaranteed to make her go crazy.

What with helping the many customers who wandered into Off the Beaten Path searching for a card or gift item, and getting some new shelves set up in the back, Megan found that the morning went quickly. She had just finished arranging a new card display when Erin walked in. "Hey, that looks nice," her roommate said, studying the multicolored cardboard stand.

Megan smiled. "We got a brand-new batch of un-greeting cards in today. They're really funny."

"Good. I'll take a look while you buy yourself some lunch."

"Are you sure you don't mind babysitting the store?"

"Not at all."

"Good," said a familiar masculine voice. "I'll use this opportunity to take Megan to lunch."

She spun around to find herself staring at the man with aquamarine eyes who haunted her daydreams. He was wearing dark slacks and a white shirt, and carrying a light-colored sports coat casually over his shoulder. The mere sight of him sent her senses spinning out of control. "Hello, Sebastian," she said finally.

"Come on," he urged, "get your purse and coat, and I'll take you someplace special."

She started to do as he'd said, but stopped abruptly as his words finally registered. Was he inviting her or issuing an order? She didn't care for his choice of words. "On second thought, I don't think I will. I have too many things to do," she told him. She sensed that the sudden chill in her tone surprised both Erin and Sebastian. Comprehension dawned in her roommate's eyes, but no such elucidation took place in Sebastian's.

"I think I'll go get myself a cup of coffee from the back," Erin mumbled, ducking out to the rear of the store.

"Would you care to explain what just happened here?" Sebastian asked. "I feel like the only one at the United Nations without an interpreter."

"I'm busy," Megan replied flatly.

Almost on cue, a tall young woman wearing designer jeans and a embroidered silk blouse strolled into the shop. "Hi, Megan."

"Hi, Cindy. How's my favorite customer?" Megan didn't have to turn around to know that Sebastian was staring. Cindy's long brown hair, highlighted by streaks of purple, was something to behold. "What can I do for you today?"

"My boyfriend Randy's birthday is coming up, and I want to get something special for him. He's so difficult to shop for, but I know he loves your store. Do you remember him? He came in with me last week when I bought several boxes of your People Crackers."

"Did his dog like them?"

"Dog?" Cindy frowned and shook her head. "We bought them for the pigeons at the park. They loved them. One pigeon became positively addicted to the ones shaped like little statues. Actually, I think they were supposed to be mailmen."

"I see," Megan said seriously.

"Anyway, I was hoping you could give me some advice on what to get for him."

"What kind of hobbies does Randy have?"

"All he ever does when he gets home from work is watch television." The young woman inspected a display of wind chimes in the far corner. "Sometimes he even watches it when it's not on. He says the empty screen helps him meditate."

Sebastian moved close behind Megan and whispered,

"Maybe someone will beam him down a gift from his home planet."

She bit her tongue to keep from laughing. Without turning to look at Sebastian, she hurried to her customer's side. "I have the perfect gift for someone who likes to watch television."

The young woman paused and pointed to a life-size suit of armor. "How much is this?"

"One hundred and fifty dollars. We got him second-hand from a couple who just moved into an apartment. They found it took up too much room. It's in excellent condition."

"But too expensive for me." Cindy sighed. "What were you going to say before I interrupted you?"

"I was going to suggest you get Randy one of our Couch Potato animals. You lean against them while you're watching television. You see, 'couch potato' is slang for someone who just sits around watching television. These animal-shaped beanbags are much more comfortable than pillows, and they make the perfect pet." Megan led Cindy to a side shelf where several of the three-foot-tall furry beanbag creatures were perched.

Cindy studied the price tag. "I can afford this. I'll take this one," she said, selecting one that resembled an overweight panda.

Megan rang up the sale. "Here you go, Cindy. I hope Randy likes it."

"I'm sure he will." She smiled enthusiastically. "I think you have the best store in town. Wait until our friends see this! I bet you'll end up selling your entire supply."

"I'll tell you what," Megan said. "In return, I'll give the VIP treatment to anyone you recommend."

"It's always so nice to come here. You make all your customers feel special."

"That's because they really are," Megan replied, waving as the young woman left the shop.

"I don't know about special, but that one's certainly strange," Sebastian commented dryly.

"Cindy's been terrific. She's sent a lot of local craftsmen to me. I need those contacts to keep my unusual merchandise in stock. What you see here—from the kitty litter made out of clay that sparkles, to the stadium parkablanket built for two—is not something I can order out of just any catalog. I really have to search to find places that can supply me with the type of items I want to carry."

"Are all your customers as eccentric as Cindy?"

"Stick around. Cindy won't seem so unusual after you meet some of the others. They aren't all as colorful as she is, but they're far from dull."

"You like them, don't you?"

"Of course, I do. I think all my customers are fascinating. Our clientele even includes the wives of several city councilmen."

"I'm impressed."

"You should be," she teased. "What you're seeing here is the beginning of an empire."

"Now that you're in a better mood, why don't you tell me the real reason why you changed your mind about having lunch with me?"

Sebastian Gladstone wasn't one to let things pass, she realized. "I didn't like the way you worded your invitation," she admitted. "I haven't taken orders from anyone in a long time, Sebastian, and I assure you I have no intention of beginning again now. I tend to balk when anyone issues an invitation as if it were a command."

His expression grew wary and speculative. "Rather touchy on the subject, aren't you?"

"Probably."

"I don't like women who criticize my behavior," he challenged bluntly.

She considered his statement. Had he expected to slip into her life and begin ordering her around? If so, he was in for some harsh enlightenment. "It looks like we've reached a standoff," she said, regarding him levelly. Her heart was pounding so hard she was afraid he'd hear it. What if he simply turned around and refused to talk to her again?

For several moments neither one spoke. Finally he broke the silence. "I'm sorry, Megan. I didn't mean to be so rude. I'll be more careful about the way I phrase things, and, to show your good will, you can buy us lunch today." His devastating smile softened his proposal.

Satisfied, she nodded. But as she turned around to pick up her purse, she remembered she had only four dollars and change left to last until the end of next week. Why had she agreed to buy *his* lunch?

There was only one solution. She'd take him to the small park located nearby and buy him the best hot dog in the city. "Come on. You're in for a treat," she said, grabbing his arm. "I have the perfect place in mind, and we won't even need a car."

As they strolled arm in arm down the crowded side-walk—Sebastian had refused to relinquish her—Megan admitted she had overreacted. But perhaps it was best to lay some ground rules right from the start. She was no child, and she had no intention of allowing him to treat her like one.

"There's our restaurant," she said, pointing ahead to a small hot dog stand in McCracken Park.

"My favorite! Tube steaks!" he exclaimed. "I suspected you were a lady who enjoyed the finer things in life."

Megan bought a hot dog and a small drink for each of them, then, leading the way, she crossed a windswept hill to a circle of eucalyptus trees on the far side. "Here we are. Luxury, courtesy of mother nature."

He laughed, and she was pleased to see that he really seemed to be enjoying himself.

She patted the ground beside her. "I hardly ever get the chance to buy someone lunch. Have a seat."

As he stretched out beside her, she was acutely aware of his long legs and powerful chest so close to her. "You're really unpredictable, you know that?" he said.

She flushed. "Not once you understand me. Then I'm completely predictable."

"I doubt it." He held her gaze warmly as he bit into his hot dog. For several minutes they ate in silence, then he leaned back against the tree trunk and watched while she consumed the last of her lunch.

Megan rolled up the wrappers and stuck them inside the paper bag, then stretched out on the ground, propped up on one elbow. "It's so nice to be outside for a change." As she raised her eyes to his, a delicious warmth seeped through her. His expression was serious, intent.

"You have a strange power over me, Megan. I can't seem to get you out of my mind."

Her heart was pounding. Her mouth was suddenly dry. How in the world was she supposed to answer that? She couldn't very well admit he'd been in her thoughts constantly, too. "There are two ways to cure that," she replied with forced lightness. "Call an exorcist or take two aspirins. Of course, if you're really desperate, you can do both."

"I enjoy thinking about *you*, you beautiful witch." His eyes caressed her warmly. "But I don't understand why you're fighting what's happening between us. Are you afraid you're too inexperienced to handle the situation?"

She was embarrassed by his shrewd observation. It was too close to the truth. In defense, she feigned indignation. "Of course not. I'm not that inexperienced. For your information, I was married."

He leaned toward her and stroked her arm lightly. "Tell me about it."

To her surprise, she realized she wanted to tell him all about it. She paused to collect her thoughts, then began. Sebastian listened carefully, his eyes never leaving her face.

"I couldn't spend the rest of my life doing what everyone else wanted me to do," Megan said finally. "When I lived with my aunt, I wasn't allowed to have even the slightest bit of fun without her approval. I couldn't date most of the boys who asked me out, since they never met her lofty standards. When I married Jim, I was so blinded by romantic fantasies that I didn't realize he was a domineering person much like my aunt. Every time I wanted to do something on my own, to go somewhere without him or the boys, he made me feel guilty or selfish. Finally, I realized I was fulfilling his dream instead of my own. I had to leave.

"I've come a long way since then, but I've still got a lot to learn about myself and about life. I want to stand on my own two feet without having to lean on someone else for support." Her voice grew stronger with conviction. "Don't assume I'm naive simply because I come from a small town and haven't been on my own for very long. As you well know, you can't live through marriage and a divorce, and remain unaffected. I carry some scars, too."

His expression was soft with understanding. "I wish I could erase those scars, Megan, but I can't. Instead, I *can* show you how good it can be between two people." He put his hands on her shoulders and pulled her toward him. She gazed dizzily into the glorious blue depths of his eyes, trembling slightly as he drew her within mere inches of an embrace. Knowing what would follow if she allowed it, she twisted gently away and brushed his cheek lightly.

She stood up and straightened her hair, avoiding his gaze. "It's time to go."

He stood up, too. "Megan, you can't ignore your feelings forever. I know part of you aches for the warmth we could share together."

Without answering, she got up and headed back. He followed. "I don't want to talk about it anymore," she said finally. "I insist that our relationship remain a business friendship and nothing more. Otherwise, we're going to create more complications than either one of us knows what to do with."

"Speak for yourself."

She stole a glance at him. His eyes captured hers, holding them for a brief instant. His knowing wink made her heart leap. She felt her face grow hot.

"Since you brought up business," he continued smoothly, "would it be convenient for me to pick up your bookkeeping ledgers today? I'll return them tomorrow evening. I'd like to drop them off at my accountant's and have him work out a profit-and-loss projection on your store for the next six months. I'll need it for my tax records."

Megan quickened her pace. Maybe he was beginning to recognize who was in charge, at least as far as her business was concerned. "I'll get them for you right away."

"There's no hurry."

Yes, she had to hurry. Every nerve in her body still tingled from his touch. Her thoughts were reeling. She had to get away and restore some measure of calm to her senses.

By the time she arrived at the shop, Megan felt as tense as a tightly coiled spring. She walked through the front entrance with a sigh of relief. "Wait here and I'll be right back," she told Sebastian.

She returned moments later with the ledgers. "Here they are. If there's anything else I can do for you, just let me know."

"You certainly can do more for me." His lazy, arrogant grin told her he was deliberately reading much more into her statement than she'd intended.

Her temper flared. "Why do you get such perverse pleasure out of teasing me? Do you think I won't fight back?" She raised her chin defiantly. "How would you like it if I started pressuring you into doing things you didn't want to do?"

"Anytime," he taunted good-naturedly. "I'm always willing to please you."

She fumed silently, frustrated by her inability to get back at him. Finally she said, "I've got to get back to work." Without another word, she stalked over to Erin, who was busy dusting one of the back shelves.

"Is he gone?" Megan whispered, not wanting to turn around to see for herself.

Erin laughed and nodded. "What's the matter? Is he getting to be too much for you?"

"I try to keep control of the situation, but the longer I'm around him, the more confused I become. I swear to myself that I'm not going to let him even touch me, then the next thing I know, I'm repeating that to myself over and over again as his arms slip around me."

"Maybe you're falling in love."

She shot her friend an exasperated glance. "No, Erin, I am *not* falling in love. I'm suffering from terminal lust, that's all."

"You keep right on saying that. You're bound to convince yourself sooner or later."

"You have a cruel streak in you, Erin." Megan took

the feather duster from her hand and continued cleaning the shelves. "What are your plans for the rest of the afternoon?"

"I'm getting together with Larry Hart, the new disc jockey at the station. He promised to take me out for dessert at Finian's Bakery."

"Let me guess. You're going to let him buy you a dozen chocolate-filled croissants and then eat yourself into a coma."

"No," Erin replied slowly, "I don't want him to think I've got a piggish appetite. He's very cute, and I'm trying to impress him with my ladylike behavior. Seven or eight croissants will be my limit."

"He'll think you eat like a bird," Megan agreed, laughing.

Erin joined in. "That's what I like about you. You're so supportive." Retrieving her purse and jacket, she gave Megan a casual wave. "I'll see you later. I'm off to meet the man of my dreams."

"With you, that means he'll be around as long as the flavor-of-the-month ice cream."

Erin shot Megan a mock scowl and left. Once more Megan turned her attention to business. After greeting two new customers, she concentrated on finding what they wanted. She was determined to forget all about Sebastian, even if only for one afternoon.

The first customer was obviously a successful businessman. Conservatively attired in a three-piece wool suit and carrying a leather portfolio, he made a predictable purchase—a role-playing game called Escape the IRS. The other customer, an elderly gentleman, bought two scale-model kits of Lady Godiva on her horse. He said one was for his brother on his eighty-second birthday, and the other one was for himself.

Despite such fun customers, Megan grew restless. Maybe the effort it took to keep her mind on business had exhausted her, but for the first time since she had opened her doors for business, she closed the shop at precisely six o'clock and went home.

She looked forward to spending Saturday night away from the store. After consuming a can of split pea soup and a large glass of orange juice, she sat down on the living room floor in front of the four-inch screen of her mini-television set.

Fantasy Boat was on. The familiar gnomelike captain was greeting the passengers on his latest cruise, a sojourn to St. Barthélemy, an island in the French West Indies, where the passengers would all become contestants in the International Shuffleboard Championship.

Unable to concentrate on the show, Megan switched to another channel. *Road Rider* was on, but a story about a guy and eight chimps who ran their own trucking company could scarcely be considered stimulating entertainment, she decided.

Tuning into a third show, she groaned. *My Mother the Condominium*. She had seen this one before. It was about a guy who managed an apartment building that had been possessed by the spirit of his dead mother.

She switched off the set. It was definitely not a night for television. Not wanting to remain idle, and thus allow herself to dwell on thoughts of Sebastian, she paced the apartment, searching restlessly for something to do.

She could clean out the refrigerator. But when she opened the door, she discovered that her roommate had beaten her to the punch, despite their deal. How nice of Erin. Even the mysterious foil-wrapped items were gone.

Megan had already read all the magazines in the apartment several times, and she didn't feel like working on a puzzle. She could call a friend, but they probably had already made plans for the evening. Darn! If she had so much restless energy, she might as well put it to good use at the store. She hadn't taken inventory for the month yet, and it would be infinitely easier to do so late at night, when there weren't any interruptions.

Megan slammed out of the house and drove to the shopping center. She let herself in through the back door, retrieved her clipboard from her desk, and got to work.

As part of a restored residence, her shop had once comprised three upstairs bedrooms. One of the adjoining walls had been removed to create a large space for the main shop. The smallest of the rooms had been left intact and now served as her office-storeroom. One exit opened onto a hallway that led directly outside to a short flight of stairs and the sidewalk. The same hallway also led to a staircase to the lower level. Megan's customers could enter and leave the shop either way, while a third hall door served as a service entrance.

As Megan began to take inventory, she noticed that the air smelled stuffy. Not wanting to run up her electric bill by switching on the air conditioner, she propped open the back door with a large, empty cardboard box, and opened a window in the hallway. Ah, fresh air, at last.

She had taken just a few steps down the corridor when a man shouted something indistinguishable from far away. She spun around—and came face to face with a gigantic Doberman pinscher staring at her through the open window! His big feet were perched on the sill, and his sharp white fangs were bared in a vicious growl. He was scrambling to get at her, as if he fully intended to tear her limb from limb.

"Help!" she cried in a thin voice, her eyes darting nervously around, desperately seeking help. Her slightest movement might make the dog jump through the opening and attack her. *I'm not afraid, I'm not afraid,* she repeated silently as sweat beaded on her brow and her hands clenched in terror. "Nice doggie. You don't want to hurt me, do you?" she whispered. Each second seemed an eternity. Then, to her relief, she heard footsteps coming toward her. "Help! Help!" she called again.

She heard running, and out of the corner of her eye she saw the far door open and a figure emerge from the shadows. "Put your hands up and don't move," a male voice ordered.

Megan turned her head slightly to see an overweight man dressed in a khaki uniform and jacket, wearing the billed cap and badge of a security guard. The gun in his hand was pointed straight at her! "Who are you? Identify yourself," he demanded.

Megan gestured with exceeding caution toward the dog. "Please tell the nice doggie to go away," she pleaded hoarsely.

"Identify yourself!" the voice boomed again. The guard took several steps closer.

"I'm Megan Lord," she answered quickly. "Sir, I think you must have me confused with someone else. I'm sorry if I startled you, but I rent the shop down the hall."

He stepped further into the light and spoke briefly into his walkie-talkie. Moments later, another man in an identical uniform entered the hallway.

Megan regarded them warily, then the dog, which was still poised in the window, salivating profusely. This was ridiculous! Why was she apologizing? She had every right to be there! It was past time she asserted herself. "Look, fellows, I belong here, but to the best of my knowledge, neither of you guys do. Now, what the heck is going on?"

"Don't even think of moving, lady," the larger man ordered. "Fritz there"—he pointed to the dog—"isn't very selective about who he tears apart."

"I'm telling you that I own—"

"Do you have any identification?" the smaller man demanded.

"Sure." She gestured toward her shop and, to her

horror, saw that the door had slammed shut. Apparently the cardboard box hadn't been heavy enough to keep it propped open. "My identification is in there," she said lamely, realizing with a sinking feeling that she was in *big* trouble.

"I don't suppose you have a key," the tall security guard said derisively.

"I do, but it's inside the shop." She could tell from their expressions that they didn't believe her.

"Sure. Just for the record, lady, how many store owners do you think come in through the window?" the tall guard said.

"I didn't come in through the window! I couldn't do a chin-up and get into the building from outside even if I wanted to." She tried to keep her voice from rising hysterically. "I didn't want to run the air conditioning," she explained reasonably, "but the window inside my store has been stuck shut since before I moved in so I decided to open the hall window"—she gestured with a toss of her head—"and prop open my back door to get some circulation." She shot them her most convincing look of wide-eyed innocence.

"Well, you can tell it to the cops downtown, lady."

"What? I'm going to be arrested? You can't do that!"

"The cops are on their way." The shorter man walked over to the dog and patted him on the head. "Good job, Fritz."

Megan began to protest, but just then a city police officer arrived. Minutes later she was being handcuffed and led to a patrol car parked by the sidewalk. She fought the tears stinging her eyes. "Why won't you listen to me?" she pleaded. "I can prove who I am if you'll only let me call my roommate. She's got a duplicate key to the shop."

"You'll get one call after we book you," the officer

replied. "You can get in touch with whoever you want then."

Without another word they hustled her into the rear of the squad car. Megan wanted to die of humiliation. This was worse than falling into Sebastian's pool. Sebastian? Wasn't that his red sports car pulling up to the curb? Shocked, Megan watched as he sprung out of the car and shook hands with the two security guards, apparently congratulating them on a job well done.

She stared helplessly at the rolled-up car window. She couldn't roll it down with handcuffs on. Should she worry about decorum? Definitely not! In as loud a voice as she could muster, she yelled out: *"Sebastian!"*

Suddenly it seemed as if a stage director had shouted "Freeze!" Sebastian turned slowly toward her. She watched his expression turn from blank puzzlement to wide-eyed disbelief. Immediately he rushed over to the car. "Megan, what are you doing here? Were you in the store when the burglar tried to break in? Are you okay?"

She tried to speak, but the words just wouldn't come. She felt as if she'd been trapped in a nightmare and was only now beginning to wake up.

"Wait a minute." Sebastian stopped speaking abruptly. "What are *you* doing in the police car?" A hint of a smile began to form on his lips as comprehension dawned. "You mean *you* got arrested in your *own* store?" He began to snicker. "Don't you know that's bad for business?"

She shot him her most withering look, the one Erin claimed killed lower forms of life at fifty paces. But it seemed to have little effect on Sebastian. His eyes were still dancing with amusement as he turned to one of the police officers, who mumbled something incomprehensible to Megan and opened the back door of the squad car. She scooted out quickly and extended her handcuffed wrists to the officer. He unlocked the manacles, apologizing profusely for the mistake and looking accusingly over his shoulder at the two embarrassed security guards.

Sebastian left her side momentarily to exchange a few quick words with them. Minutes later, the police drove away in their squad car, and the guards returned to their duties, the leashed dog at their sides calm now. Sebastian returned to Megan and placed a consoling arm across her shoulders.

"Don't you touch me, you sadist," she snapped, pulling away. "You were going to let them take me away. And then you had the gall to make fun of me because I had been arrested. I doubt if I'll ever speak to you again!"

"Wait a minute!" he protested. "It's not my fault the security guards picked you up. I notified you about the newly installed patrols. You should have called ahead to tell them you were coming."

"Called ahead?" She clenched her jaw. "Why would I call ahead when you never told me about them?"

"What do you mean? I sent everyone a letter—" He stopped abruptly. "Oh, damn!"

Looking sheepish, he pulled an envelope from his pocket and held it out to her. "I mailed the others, but I kept yours, intending to hand deliver it today at lunch. It must have slipped my mind."

Glaring, she tore open the envelope and read: "As new owner, I have retained the services of the Ace Security Agency, whose security men will be conducting regular nightly patrols of the buildings. These teams will also employ fully trained guard dogs. I hope that their presence will be an effective deterrent to the recent rash of burglaries in our neighborhood. If you require access to your store after regular hours, please inform my office or notify the security service in advance of your arrival."

Megan looked up and gave Sebastian an icy stare. "A little late, isn't it?"

"Megan, I am sorry. How can I make it up to you?"

"You might consider going for a stroll in a lion's cage. Or does flogging sound more palatable? I'll be happy to operate the whip." Still angry, she couldn't resist needling him. But in an odd way, she was pleased by the thought that he had been so preoccupied with her during lunch that he had forgotten to give her the envelope. Maybe he *did* care about her more than she'd thought.

"Why don't you take me to my own car so I can go home," she suggested. "You can make up for this fiasco by taking me out to lunch at a fancy restaurant the first chance you get."

"It's a deal," he agreed, helping her into his car. "I know all this has been difficult, so, to even out the score, I promise I won't say a word about your Minah B. Lunder account."

Megan blanched. She had been so preoccupied earlier today that she'd turned the books over to him without thinking. How could she have forgotten Minah?

She gave him a sheepish smile. "You won't believe this, but that was intended to be only a stopgap measure until I had time to properly balance the ledgers. You notice I was only a few dollars off."

"Forgive me for laughing at your being arrested, and I'll promise not to tease you unmercifully."

"Do I have a choice?"

"None at all," he said firmly.

CHAPTER FOUR

MEGAN SLEPT THROUGH most of Sunday. It was three P.M. by the time she tossed back the covers and slipped out of bed. Rubbing her eyes, she stumbled into the kitchen.

Erin greeted her cheerfully. "You look awful."

"Thanks."

Erin set a cup of coffee in front of her. "I had the most interesting phone conversation this morning. A shopping center owner claimed I was sharing an apartment with a burglary suspect. He wanted to know how his favorite criminal was doing."

Megan choked on her coffee. "Doesn't that man ever let up? And if you don't stop, I'll report you to the authorities, with whom I am now well acquainted."

Erin rinsed out her coffee cup and placed it in the drain rack. "Don't give it another thought. I'm on my way out now. Oh, by the way, is your mug shot at the post office yet?" Megan scowled at Erin, who merely laughed and left the apartment.

Megan sighed. Today she was going to relax. She'd start with a long, luxurious bubble bath, and see where her desires took her from there.

In the bathroom she ran hot water in the tub, adding a liberal amount of Erin's specially scented bath foam. Ah, the pleasures of an unhurried afternoon.

Megan had just lowered herself into the hot, sudsy water, when, to her dismay, she heard voices in the living room! She recognized Erin's right away, but it was impossible to identify the soft, masculine tones of whoever was with her. If only he'd speak up.

"Megan?" Erin called.

"I'm in the tub," she shouted back, slightly embarrassed because of their unknown visitor.

Footsteps approached the door. "Can I come in for a second?" Erin asked.

"Sure."

She peered inside the doorway. "Guess what? I found a real cute guy wandering about the halls, looking rather lost, so I decided to bring him home to you. I'm leaving now, so you two have fun."

"No, wait Erin!" But Megan's unpredictable roommate had already closed the door. Seconds later, Megan heard the apartment door slam shut.

Surely Erin was joking. She couldn't have brought a total stranger to their apartment and left him there with her sitting in the tub!

Heavier footsteps approached the bathroom door. Megan held her breath, fighting an urge to sink beneath the cloud of concealing bubbles.

"Megan?"

It was Sebastian! Damn that Erin!

"Hello," Megan called, trying to sound casual, as if

nothing unusual were happening. If he sensed her embarrassment, he was bound to take advantage of the situation.

"I came over to apologize again for last night," he explained through the door. "I wanted to make sure you were all right and didn't bear any grudges." He paused before adding provocatively, "Why don't I join you? It's not easy talking through this door, and we do want to learn everything about each other." His huskily voiced suggestion sent a warm flush across her skin, despite the rapidly cooling water.

She gasped for breath as her imagination ran wild. Did she dare ask him in? He'd undress slowly before her, revealing every inch of his magnificent physique, then step into the warm water. Their bodies would touch, their passion explode in a fierce burst of sensations...

"Shall I construe your silence as an invitation?" he asked softly.

She jumped, startled out of her daydream. "Absolutely not!" she cried, fighting sudden panic. "You should have called first. It's very rude to just barge in like this." She stopped abruptly, struggling to regain her cool.

"Megan," he said, "I'm trying very hard *not* to barge in on you."

"Don't you dare! I'll be out in a minute," she called frantically, scrubbing herself furiously. "Wait for me in the living room."

"If you're sure."

"I'm sure."

Megan felt hopelessly Victorian, but she simply couldn't get out of that tub until she was sure he was far away from the bathroom door. Don't be silly, she chided herself. He doesn't have X-ray vision. Maybe not, her other half argued, but he did have a thoroughly unnerving ability to read her thoughts. And she herself seemed to have little control over them lately.

Megan rinsed off, hopped out of the tub, quickly toweled herself dry, put on her bra and panties, then pulled on old jeans and a white crocheted pullover. Standing in front of the mirror, she brushed her hair and arranged it around her shoulders in a simple style.

She couldn't put off her grand entrance into the living room any longer. She took a deep breath. Her hands felt cold, and her mouth was dry. She opened the door and tiptoed down the hall into the adjoining room. She glanced around. Where was he? "Sebastian?"

"In here," he called from the kitchen. "I've been looking at your puzzle."

Oh, no! Steeling herself, she peeked around the corner. He looked up, grinning broadly. "At first I assumed the puzzle was Erin's. Then I saw her note to you on the box."

Megan thought she might strangle from lack of air. "It was a joke," she explained nervously. "I certainly didn't expect her to get something like that for me. Of course, the only reason she got it was because she knows certain things embarrass me very easily." Her eyes darted nervously around the room, looking at everything except the puzzle.

"Which 'certain things'?" he asked mischievously. "I have to know what embarrasses you if I'm supposed to avoid mentioning them."

"Oh, give me a break," Megan pleaded, thoroughly exasperated. "You know." Without thinking, she began washing a glass in the sink. Anything to avoid Sebastian's twinkling eyes.

"But I'm not sure," he insisted, crossing the kitchen in two quick strides and stopping directly behind her. He slipped his arms around her waist and forced her back against him, molding her curves to his masculine length. Electric shocks tingled along her scalp and down her spine, setting off a similar response in her very depths.

"Good Lord!" She dropped the dishcloth as he pressed her buttocks harder against him. Her pulse skyrocketed as his arms tightened. How could she escape his grasp without making a fool of herself? Did she even *want* to escape it? Didn't she *want* to keep their relationship light and casual? All of a sudden she felt very confused. His touch was so inviting, tempting her beyond endurance . . .

"Ummm, you smell good," he murmured close to her ear. His lips brushed her neck, the warmth of his breath sending shivers of pure pleasure skittering along her nerve endings. Halfheartedly, she tried to free herself of his embrace, but his arms locked even tighter, crushing her against his hard frame.

He inched his hand under her sweater, delicately seeking her soft skin. The contact enveloped her senses in a shower of sparks that left her feeling giddy and intoxicatingly helpless. Reason was telling her to stop, but instinctively she arched her back and rested her head against his shoulder. His palm seared her skin as it roamed freely.

Unhooking the front opening of her bra, he lifted the sheer material away from her breasts. He nuzzled her neck and sensuously continued to caress the skin above and just below her breasts.

She yearned for his touch to explore further, to be engulfed by his strength, but he continued at his own slow pace. He seemed to take pleasure in the small cries that rose from her throat, his own response growing ever more fiery in reaction to hers.

"Please," she managed in a raw voice. "Please don't tease me."

"And what would you have me do, my beautiful Megan?" he whispered. "Tell me."

She felt the beat of her heart and the hardness of his manhood pressing against her. He wanted her! The words hammered in her brain, the knowledge seducing her with a force she hadn't dreamed possible. This wonderfully virile man wanted *her!*

"I need you to touch me," she whispered. "Please!" Her hand closed over his. Relishing the voluptuous sensations his palm imprinted on her skin, she moved his fingers to her breast and pressed them against her. "Here."

His thumb made a lazy circle over her hard nipple, each rotation branding her sensitive skin like a hot iron. "Who's bewitched whom, I wonder?" he murmured softly. "I love the way you melt against me. Your body is so soft and yielding." Gently he turned her around in the circle of his arms.

She parted her lips, scarcely aware of what she was doing. A burning hunger consumed her, demanding satisfaction. As his fingers tightened around the honey-brown center of her breast, she gasped. A small cry of passion drowned in her throat as his mouth descended, taking hers with a mastery that left her quivering in his arms. His tongue invaded her mouth, assaulting her senses, compelling her to lower her last defenses. Deepening the kiss, he continued to savor the exquisite pleasures she offered.

His breath was ragged as he left her mouth in search of other discoveries. He blazed an incendiary trail on her flesh as his lips descended and encircled the taut centers of her breasts, his tongue making a thorough exploration of her aching nipples.

Megan was being driven by a longing too powerful to resist. She tangled her fingers in his hair and pressed him against her, crying out softly in her need.

His response was primitive and instinctive. "Yes, Megan! Give yourself to me." He buried his lips at her waist, tasting her with a languor that wrenched the air from her lungs.

His hands slipped to the waistband of her jeans. He unfastened them and pushed them downward. Chill air struck her lace-covered hips as his hand drifted ever so slowly toward the apex of her thighs.

This was madness! She had to stop! But every nerve cried out, demanding her surrender. She needed him. She wanted to become one with this man who had awakened such overwhelming feeling in her. The struggle inside her reached fevered intensity as his palm cupped and caressed her.

She struggled against the passion that sent searing tendrils of heat to her very core. Things were happening too fast. She wasn't in control of herself; she had to stop this rashness before she did something she would regret. "I want you, but I'm not ready for this," she finally burst out.

It was as if he hadn't heard her. His mouth found hers once more in a savage kiss. She fell against him, needing the support of his strong body to keep from falling into a limp heap at his feet. Still, his lips refused to release her, straying only to the side of her mouth, where they sampled the sweet softness there.

A startled cry passed her lips before the sound was swallowed by his mouth. His nimble fingers turned her body liquid. She had no strength to fight him.

"Tell me you want me," he demanded softly.

"No!" She shook her head, clinging to him in desperation. "It's too soon for this to happen." She couldn't utter the words he wanted to hear. She couldn't let him make love to her. The independence she'd fought so hard to achieve was being threatened as never before.

His eyes bored into hers. "Megan, don't pull away from me. I care about you. Give in to your feelings. I know you want me. Give yourself to me, sweetheart!"

"No!" She was being torn in two! "You don't understand."

He eased his hold on her, but she sensed his growing perplexity . . . and his rising anger. "You're right, Megan, I don't understand. But I want to." His voice was gently persuasive. "Tell me what I need to know."

The words went straight to her heart and fed the embers of desire still burning there. She knew now, without any doubt, that her feelings for Sebastian went beyond mere physical passion. The warmth that enveloped her every time she saw him had as much to do with love as with desire. But how could it have happened so fast?

"I can't allow my emotions to override my common sense," she told him. "I need to be independent to keep growing. Before I get involved with anyone, I have to know who I am and what I'm capable of accomplishing on my own."

He gave a deep sigh. Then, without a word, he refastened the front opening of her bra and helped her smooth her clothing back into place. "I've never been a patient man, Megan," he said finally, "but maybe it's time I learned that certain things in life can't be rushed. I'll give you as much time as you need. But I think you're fighting yourself as well as me." He lifted her chin with one finger, forcing her to look at him. "But maybe that's just as well. You have to discover your own feelings before you can care about me. In the end I think we'll be together, even if it takes you a while to find out what's really important to you."

She moved away from his touch and stepped back. "I thought I was the one who daydreamed a lot," she said, hiding how close he had come to the truth about her feelings. "I'm attracted to you, Sebastian, but that's all. Don't read more into it. You expect too much from me."

She shook her head and continued, unable to stem the flow of words. "Do you realize how little we have in common? We come from completely different backgrounds. You socialize with a rich, sophisticated crowd that's completely out of my league. You go to operas and ballets. I stay home and watch television because I can't afford to go out. You like me because I'm different, but once the newness wears off, you'll be bored with me. Then it would be only a matter of time before you found a woman you had more in common with."

Still she babbled on, the flow of words becoming an uncontrollable torrent. "I didn't spend this last year and a half struggling to establish a life for myself just so I could have an affair. No thanks. I can live without the pain and self-doubt *that* would bring."

Sebastian looked concerned as he stepped forward and raised a hand to touch her cheek, his caress subduing her gently. "All I want is a chance for us to get to know each other," he said quietly. "Spend the afternoon with me. I came here hoping to make up for last night, but now I see that what we really need is a chance to spend some time together, to learn to trust each other. I don't want to hurt you or take away your independence, Megan." He held out his hand. "Come with me?"

He looked so sincere, how could she resist? Maybe she could win his simple friendship. Maybe she *could* convince him it would be best for both of them to keep their relationship on a safe plane. Maybe just this once, she thought, she'd be able to take charge of a situation that involved Sebastian and have it go precisely the way she wanted it to.

He slipped his arm around her waist as they went downstairs to his car. "Sebastian, where are we going?"

"I thought I'd take you where we can have a long, uninterrupted talk. Not my house, though," he added hastily at her warning look. "What we need is a quiet spot on neutral territory. Any suggestions?"

"Golden Gate Park has over one thousand acres. Surely we can find a place to talk there."

"Good idea. How about a walk around the dunes on Fort Funston? We'll stay away from the hang-gliding area."

She nodded, feeling some of the tension leave her body. "I think you're right. It should be nice at this time of day. Most of the hikers will be leaving, so we'll have all the privacy we want."

They fell silent as Sebastian maneuvered his sports car through the traffic, heading toward the southern end of San Francisco County. He kept his eyes on the road. Megan stared out the passenger window, trying to get her thoughts in order. She was startled out of her reverie when Sebastian spoke. "Megan, something you said really bothers me. Do you really think I'm going to hurt you? People have misunderstood my intentions before, but never so completely."

"I don't think you would intentionally," she answered, "but eventually that's what would happen. Have you ever really thought about how different our lives are? In comparison to yours, mine is painfully dull. You live in an exciting world of complex business deals and fast society. I have only a tiny little shop filled with bizarre items."

He frowned thoughtfully. "Megan, my life isn't really as exciting as you make it seem. Nor is yours as dull. You're the first woman I've met in years that I've been interested in. It's refreshing to be with someone who says what she really means. I know where I stand with you. All I have to do is look into your eyes, and I can practically see what you're thinking. There's a freshness about you. I see it in the way you talk, in the way you dress, and in just about everything you do. It's your simple honesty that attracts me to you."

She couldn't doubt his own honesty at that moment. But the thought that he might really care about her seemed too good to be true. "Sebastian," she began, "I've often been accused of seeing things the way I'd like them to be, rather than the way they are. I think that's exactly what you're doing with me. Your fantasy of me is preventing you from seeing me as I really am. I'm not naive, inexperienced, or any of those adjectives you keep using to describe me. But I *am* new to the city and to the single, independent life I'm living. I came from being a housewife, responsible for two boys who could have been my brothers, to a strange city where I had to become self-supporting for the first time in my life. I proved I could adjust to all that. I'm hardly a child."

"I never said you were," he protested. "Why do you react as though I'm maligning you when I say you haven't been around much? It's a fact. You may have known pain, Megan, but you're scarcely what I would call worldly. You remind me of a rose about to open. You're full of promise. By your own admission, you've never even been in love, though you may have thought you were at the time. Why are you so afraid of finding the love you've dreamed about—maybe with me?"

How wonderful his words made her feel! But she was so confused...

"It's hard for me to explain this," she began, "but I want you to understand. You're a threat to me because I don't want to fall in love right now, and I'm afraid I might. I enjoy being self-sufficient. My life isn't perfect, but it's *mine*. I've never been able to say that before. I don't want to lose that sense of being my own person. I've worked so hard to get it!"

She paused, then added, "Also, I really believe what I told you before. To you, I'm different. You've admitted that's partly why you're attracted to me. What happens when you grow used to me?"

"I'm drawn to you because of who you are, not just because you're different. You're beautiful, Megan, but also sensitive. There's a vulnerability about you that makes me want to take you in my arms. I don't want anyone or anything to hurt you. I just want to be with you. Is that so wrong?"

He was pulling her heartstrings like a puppeteer working the strings of a puppet. She could not resist him. "No, it's not so wrong," she said, barely audibly. "But that isn't the way I want it to be between us."

They'd been driving in the park for several minutes. Now he pulled the car over to the side of the road and came to a stop. "Let's go for a walk," he suggested. At her nod, he helped her out.

Hand in hand, they approached a line of sand dunes and followed it along the shoreline until they came to a secluded spot shaded by a cluster of pine trees. In silent agreement they sat down on the green dune grass that had pushed up through the sand. Megan stared out to sea, letting the wind catch and lift her hair, listening to the soothing roll of the surf and the cries of wheeling gulls.

At last Sebastian said quietly, "If you could change one thing about our relationship, what would it be?"

"Me mostly." She stretched out on her side, propping herself up on one elbow. "Actually, I *am* in the process of changing, which is another reason why I don't want to get involved with anyone right now. I need more time to grow. I want to be a woman who can self-confidently take charge of any situation. For instance," she added shyly, "instead of waiting for you to make the romantic overtures and set the pace, I'd like to occasionally take the lead myself."

"Are you saying that my sexual aggressiveness brings out the passive side of your nature, the very part of you you're hoping to outgrow?"

She nodded slowly. "Yes, that's part of it."

He lay down on his back, his hands locked beneath his head for support, and stared thoughtfully into the sky. "Let's pretend that at this very moment you're exactly the woman you're hoping to become. You can set the pace for us. You can do anything you'd like to do without being afraid. What would you do that you haven't done already?"

She stared at the sandy ground. "I don't know."

He glanced at her, then refocused on the gulls overhead. "Think about it then. How would you handle the situation right now?"

She smiled, toying with the idea in her imagination. That was simple. She'd lean over him and kiss him deeply. She'd drink in the heady masculine taste of him, then shatter his control, making him want and need her more than life itself. She sighed.

He chuckled. "I see you've had an idea. What is it?"

Her face grew hot under his steady scrutiny. Now what had she gotten herself into? "I can't tell you."

He laughed more loudly. "If you really want to continue to grow and change, Megan, you're going to have to be braver. Then again, maybe you're not ready to take the initiative," he teased. "It could be that, for all your talk of wanting to be aggressive, part of you still longs to be dominated."

Her temper flared at his chauvinistic suggestion. Is that what he thought? Well, she'd show him. The last thing she needed was a domineering, know-it-all man!

"Maybe it's the other way around," she suggested coyly. "Have you considered that maybe it's *you* who wants to be dominated? I think that's the real reason you're so intent on goading me. Hmm." She pursed her lips and narrowed her eyes speculatively. "Why don't we put my theory to the test?"

CHAPTER FIVE

SHE LEANED OVER him and slowly brought her mouth to his. In her daydreams she had always remained cool and remote, able to topple his restraint without losing control. But now, as she felt his warm, hard body beneath her, a sharp wave of desire enveloped her. It was only a kiss, she told herself, but the message failed to reach her rapidly spinning senses.

His arms tightened about her waist, crushing her to him, and Megan sensed his will to dominate. This was no fantasy! The emotions she had aroused were primitive and fierce. Greedily she bent again to drink from his parted lips.

"Oh, Megan!" he uttered hoarsely, tangling his fingers in her hair and pressing her lips urgently to his. The ache throbbing in the pit of her stomach clamored to be assuaged. She would never be whole again until Sebastian made love to her...

The thought frightened her back to a cold realization of where she was and what she was doing. She pushed Sebastian gently away and held his eyes with hers, hoping that somehow the contact would help him understand. "Sebastian, we've got to stop." She sat upright, hugging her knees to her chest. "I feel as if I'm fighting a war with myself, constantly torn between the need to deepen my involvement with you and the need to retain my freedom." A cold breeze blew, and she shivered. "I think we'd better go back."

Sebastian stood and helped her up, then slipped off his jacket and wrapped it around her shoulders. "This will help you keep warm."

"But *you'll* be cold," she protested.

He laughed lightly. "Don't give it a thought. A cold breeze may be just what I need—the next best thing to a cold shower."

She was glad he had a sense of humor and wasn't angry with her. She didn't mean to lead him on, though it must look that way. "Your chivalry makes me feel guilty," she admitted. "Since we're closer to your house than to my apartment, why don't we make a quick stop there? You can get another jacket, and I won't worry about your catching pneumonia."

"All right." He met her eyes for an instant. "To be honest, it is a little too brisk for my taste."

He kept his arm around her shoulders as they returned to the car. The warmth of his body so close to hers sent a rush of renewed awareness coursing through her. She wanted him all over again. She marveled at how such powerful feelings could be aroused from such a simple touch. How would she ever learn to control her desire for him?

She stole a furtive glance at him. Oh, how she wanted

him! A mental picture flashed through her mind. Dressed in a black negligee, she was arousing and teasing him until she unleashed the animal passions he held barely in check. Whispering her name over and over in a raw voice that quaked with desire, he finally joined his body with hers, releasing an explosion of sensations.

"You have a very sensual expression on your face," he said quietly, startling her. "What are you thinking?"

"I . . ."

"Megan." He shook his head in frustration. "If only you could see inside me and know how much you mean to me. Maybe then you'd believe that what I'm offering you wouldn't be a prison."

He opened the door to his car and helped her inside, then slid behind the wheel and started the engine. The trip to his home took less than ten minutes, but this time his driving seemed restrained. Megan saw no signs of playfulness as he sped up and down the hills of San Francisco.

The deafening silence between them remained unbroken until they parked in his driveway and he invited her inside. He led the way to the den, where Megan made herself comfortable on the sofa.

"I need a brandy to warm up," he said, heading for the bar. "Would you like something?"

"Brandy would be fine."

He returned holding two partially filled snifters and sat down next to her. Too close for comfort, she thought with some alarm. He met her gaze over the rim of his glass as they sipped the fiery amber liquid. "Megan, I wish there was some way I could rip away the barriers you've erected between us."

The full impact of his undisguised desire hit her like a blow. She looked away. "Sebastian, don't make it any more difficult than it already is for me."

"I want to make it difficult for you, Megan," he insisted. "I want to make it impossible for you not to care for me as much as I care for you. I would never take away the freedom and identity that you've discovered for yourself. If I were to mold you into someone else, then the Megan I care about wouldn't exist. I hope someday you'll believe me."

A shiver ran up her spine. She felt the warmth of his friendship and the comfort of his touch as he gently caressed her cheek.

She closed her eyes and imagined his arms around her. She remembered a scene from a book she had read years ago. Thinking her lover had left her behind, the heroine had given up all hope of happiness. Then she had seen him standing at the end of the airport corridor, his arms stretched out to her. Megan sighed. She could visualize their embrace vividly.

As she opened her eyes she realized that Sebastian, too, was holding her in his arms. Being there felt so natural and right that she didn't protest, but just nestled further into his comforting embrace.

Then, as she looked up at him, her confused feelings suddenly became unscrambled. Being in his arms now was exactly what she wanted. She *did* want to make love with Sebastian. He was a sincere, desirable, caring person, and she felt more for him than she had ever felt for any other man. Her lips parted in silent invitation, her eyes meeting his in expectation.

He pressed her against him and caressed the skin below her breasts. He seemed to read her thoughts. "Megan, I'm aching for you. Tell me you want me to make love to you, sweetheart. Tell me what I see in your eyes."

"Yes, Sebastian, make love to me," she whispered in a voice that hardly sounded like her own.

Her words seemed to enflame his masculine desire. His kiss exploded against her mouth; his searching tongue demanded a response. A tidal wave of emotion engulfed her. She tried to fit herself to his length, to meld her body to his. Instinctively, she arched against him.

"I want this to be everything you ever dreamed of, Megan," he murmured. "I want to fulfill all your fantasies and know that from this day on, I've become part of you. I want you always to remember the sweetness of your surrender to me." His whispered words seemed to sear her flesh.

He stood up and lifted her gently in his arms. She nestled against him as he carried her up the stairs. Burying her lips against his neck, she fumbled with the buttons on his shirt and slipped her hand inside to explore his firm, muscular chest. He kicked open the door to his bedroom and entered, holding her like a fragile possession as he set her on her feet beside the bed. Sweet yearning engulfed her. His eyes never left her face as he ran his palms down the length of her body in a slow, thorough exploration.

She began to tremble. He pulled her sweater over her head and allowed it to fall to the floor. The rest of her garments followed until she stood completely naked before him. She felt exposed, vulnerable, yet the desire that pulsated deep inside compelled her to seek the circle of his arms.

He held her tenderly, raining kisses over her face and cheeks. "Yes, sweetheart, cling to me. Melt your softness against me. I want to feel your touch."

His slacks felt rough against her bare skin. Frustrated by the barrier of his clothing, she gently coaxed him backward onto the bed. Fumbling with the buttons of his shirt, she opened them one by one, her senses reeling as she bared his torso.

She ran her palms down the center of his body, reveling in the way his flesh quivered beneath her touch. A groan rose from his throat as she trailed her lips in the wake of her fingers.

She sensed his struggle for restraint as he clasped her waist and shoulders and shifted her beneath him. His mouth closed over the darkened center of her breast as his flickering tongue awakened her exhilarated flesh.

She loved his masculine scent and taste, the way he made her body burn with desire. She reveled in the strength of the muscled shoulders beneath her fingers. His mouth was ravenous, flooding her senses with pleasure. She was lost to everything but the intoxicating texture of his virile body pressed tightly against hers.

Moaning softly, she twisted beneath him. "I want you, Sebastian. Oh, I do want you!"

His mouth met hers again as, in one swift movement, he thrust boldly into her. He filled her completely, exciting her beyond her wildest imaginings. Her fingers locked tightly in his hair as she surrendered to him. Together they moved in a powerful rhythm, in a crescendo of feeling that surpassed physical arousal. Megan felt bonded to Sebastian with her soul as much as with her body.

At last they cried out in unison, achieving the final release simultaneously. Megan welcomed his weight on her as, trembling in the aftermath of passion, they lay coupled in each other's arms. Sebastian rested his head between her breasts.

"Megan, was I too rough? I should have taken more care, but I wanted you so much, I couldn't stop myself." He lifted his face to look down at her. "I've never known a woman who could make me lose all control. I couldn't even think. All I knew was that I had to make you mine."

He rolled to his side, taking her with him. Megan burrowed deep in his arms. "Sebastian, it was beautiful," she assured him. "Feeling as if I was part of you, loving you and letting you love me, was the most wonderful experience in my life."

But even as she acknowledged the depth of her response, regret and confusion assailed her once again. How could she have let her feelings carry her away? "Oh, Sebastian, I can't handle a relationship like this," she cried. "My feelings frighten me too much. We went further than we should have. I don't know what happened. You seem to drive away all my common sense." She grasped his shoulders. "Promise me you'll help me keep it from happening again."

He shook his head. "No, Megan. We really care for each other, darling." He brushed his lips against her forehead. "Don't be frightened. Concentrate on what's right between us, and let your heart guide you."

"You're placing too much importance on what we just said and did in a moment of passion." She moved away from him and sat up, trying to make sense of her contradictory impulses.

Reaching out, he stroked the skin of her lower back. Megan shivered. "Don't waste your time trying to tell me you don't care about me, sweetheart. The way you respond to my touch tells me everything I need to know."

She clutched the sheet to her breasts and turned to face him. "But I don't want to become involved with anyone!"

He chuckled. "It's a little late for that, Megan. If making love isn't being 'involved,' I don't know what is!"

"Oh, you!" Half angrily, half playfully, she pulled a clump of hair on his chest. "Take that, you ogre!"

"Ouch! Cut that out!" Sebastian grabbed her wrist and twisted it behind her back, but she attacked him with the other hand. "Megan, you minx, stop that!"

"No, I won't," she exclaimed pertly. "That's what you get for getting me all hot and bothered and then taking advantage of me by making me want to go to bed with you." She pulled lightly on the hair that curled around his nipples.

"Megan..." he warned. In a swift movement, he trapped her other hand and tumbled her onto her back, then stretched out half on top of her. "Megan," he said sternly, "I won't assume full responsibility for our making love. You wanted it, too. Now, be a mature adult woman and admit it."

Her expression sobered. "You're right. It's important that I accept my share of the responsibility. But somehow I feel as if I've made a terrible mistake."

"No, Megan." He kept his eyes steady on her. "You've simply expressed your own needs in a new and very exciting way. You're a woman, and today you acted like one. It's a big step for you, and a very important one."

She considered his words. Maybe he was right. Maybe she was frightened not because he was threatening her independence, but because the world of sexual intimacy with a man who aroused both passion and caring in her was so new and bewildering to her.

Was she in love with Sebastian Gladstone? It felt like love, but she had thought she loved Jim Lord, too, and she really hadn't. She'd known Sebastian such a short time. She couldn't help but blush when she considered how short a time! How had she, modest, cautious Megan Lord, arrived in bed with virile, handsome Sebastian Gladstone so fast?

No, it couldn't be love she felt for Sebastian yet. But it might grow into love, and she couldn't allow that to happen. She was so confused already; true love would complicate the situation unbearably!

"What are you thinking?" he murmured close to her ear, his warm breath tickling her neck.

"How confused I am, and how I don't want to think about that right now."

He chuckled deep in his throat. "Then we won't think about it. We'll make love instead."

She surrendered willingly to his embrace, to the fiery

kisses he showered upon her fevered forehead, her closed eyelids, her burning cheeks, and arched throat.

That night was pure magic for her. Sebastian was strong and gentle, an expert but sensitive lover who wrapped her in mystical clouds of well-being and took her to unchartered worlds time and time again. They made love slowly and gently, then lay silently in each other's arms until they drifted contentedly off to sleep.

When the alarm clock rang at seven o'clock the next morning, Megan found she wasn't at all tired. She dressed hurriedly. "I'd better get back to my apartment so I can shower and change. I've got to open the store by ten."

"Have breakfast with me first," he urged, slipping into his underwear.

She paused momentarily, fascinated by the sight of him as he finished dressing. He was everything she could ever hope for in a man. If only she could have met him a few years from now, when she was ready for romantic involvement. "I can tell you're going to cause all sorts of trouble for me," she said quietly.

He was standing in front of the mirror, combing his hair. For a brief second their eyes met in the reflection. "I'll be thinking of you all the time, too."

She smiled. "Good."

"It isn't easy for me either, Megan. You've turned my life upside down." He placed his arm around her waist and led her downstairs, their hips bumping softly. "After Ann and I were divorced, I swore I'd never need anyone again. Love made me feel too vulnerable. I swore that if ever I found myself seriously attracted to anyone, I'd run like hell." He gave her a teasing wink. "I didn't quite make it, did I?"

"You really hoped to go through the rest of your life without caring for anyone special?" She watched carefully for his reaction, sensing the hurt behind his words.

"When I was a little boy"—he gestured for her to

take a chair behind the breakfast bar—"my father told me that a Gladstone has to be completely self-reliant. We could have friends, but we should never trust or love other people so deeply that we became emotionally dependent on them. Our position in the community demanded that we remain above reproach in both our private and business lives. Our personal involvements must never threaten that absolute standard. My father wore his pride and self-respect like a badge.

"My parents loved me, I know that," Sebastian went on. "But there were times when I chafed under my father's high and inflexible expectations. Sometimes I longed to renounce my name and escape the weight of responsibility it thrust upon me. I attended the top schools, had the most qualified teachers, and enjoyed the best of everything—all to ensure I would become a perfect Gladstone. Sometimes I wonder how I ever survived. My father was an unrelenting taskmaster. If I wasn't in top form at whatever I did, I was sure to hear about it. Then, as I got older, I began to understand what he meant about never depending on other people too much."

Sebastian paused to fill a basket with croissants and set it in front of Megan, then filled the automatic coffeemaker. He sat down again and tore off a piece of a croissant. "When I decided to leave the family business and go out on my own, Dad was furious. He even sided with Ann when she refused to go along with my plans. Then, when he realized he couldn't stop me, he simply settled a sum of money on me and told me I could never count on him for another dime. Believe me, he meant it. For better or worse, I was on my own."

Not wanting to break the flow of his thoughts, Megan remained silent as Sebastian filled their coffee cups. "Ann and I were never really close, but I was deeply hurt when she refused to accept my invitation to leave the family. I felt betrayed. I had counted on her support, but she turned away from me just when I needed her most. Obviously the money meant more to her than I did. She divorced me and married one of my father's more affluent competitors.

"From that day on, I became very cautious about the people I became emotionally attached to. Especially women. There's been no one serious . . . until you."

Megan was deeply moved by his story. She jumped up from her chair and threw her arms around his neck. "Oh, Sebastian, you shouldn't have decided to trust me." She burrowed against his chest. "You've picked the wrong person! I would never knowingly hurt you, but I haven't anything to offer but friendship. I can't make any promises or guarantees. I'm not even sure I can handle an intimate relationship! You shouldn't trust me at all."

"Megan, calm down," he said, chuckling lightly at her emotional outburst. He took her wrists from behind his head. "Megan, so far I trust you always to speak what's in your heart. Do you understand now why I value your honesty? Trust doesn't come easily to me, but I'm not in a hurry. We have a lot to offer each other, but we need time to let that trust grow." He tilted her chin up and brought his mouth down on hers in a light, questing kiss that seemed to touch the very depths of her soul.

The telephone's strident ring broke the magic mood. Sebastian released Megan and, muttering an oath, picked up the receiver. Megan heard something thump on the front doorstep and glanced questioningly at Sebastian. "Newspaper," he mouthed.

She went to retrieve it and, finishing the last of her croissant, leafed through the pages. All at once she saw a picture of Sebastian! She peered closely at the shot of him shaking hands with a man at what looked like a formal business gathering. Underneath, the caption read: "Charles Aldridge, president of Marlboro College, thanks Sebastian Gladstone, major stockholder of Excel Electronics, a supplier of computer manufacturers, for his generous donation of $50,000 to the College Scholarship Fund. The gift has been earmarked for students majoring in computer science."

It pleased Megan to know that Sebastian was sensitive to the needs of people less fortunate than himself. She was smiling as he hung up the receiver and turned to her. "What in the world are you grinning about?"

She showed him the picture. "I'm impressed."

"Is that so?" he taunted gently. "Maybe I should give money away more often—and learn to take advantage of the good feelings that generates." He stepped closer and bent to nibble her ear. "Don't I deserve a reward for my generosity?"

Laughing, Megan backed away. "Absolutely not. We haven't got time for that. You have to drive me home so we can both get to work on time."

"Spoilsport." He was chuckling as he followed her out to the car.

CHAPTER SIX

MEGAN GLANCED AT her watch. It had been only a few hours since she'd last seen Sebastian, but she already missed him. She shook her head. She was hopeless. With her thoughts on him, she had scarcely managed to get any paperwork done that morning. Chiding herself for her lack of discipline, she got up to pour herself a cup of coffee. Well, it was just about time to put things away, anyway. In another twenty minutes she'd have to open her doors for business.

As she began to restore some semblance of order to her desk, her thoughts drifted back to Sebastian. A warm glow enveloped her as she recalled their special time together. He had been so gentle, so loving...

She remembered his photograph in the newspaper. How generous of him to give money for a scholarship fund. But when she returned to her seat and stared at the low numbers in her checkbook, she couldn't help wishing someone would start a scholarship fund for her.

As the thought lingered, disturbing questions began to occur to her. Hadn't Sebastian told her he was struggling to make it in the business world just like she was? That he needed the additional income a rent increase would bring? How could he afford to give away $50,000 if that all was true? And if he didn't need the money, how could he continue to take the meager profits of her store and others like hers? He'd seen her accounting books. He knew how hard she was struggling to make ends meet.

The explanation was obvious. When it came to business, Sebastian's softer feelings had no bearing. He became coldly calculating. He felt no qualms about taking crucial money from her pocket and giving it away to someone else, just to build his image in the community. Apparently he didn't care for her as much as he'd claimed.

She slammed her fist down on the desk. To her chagrin, her coffee mug flew into the air and fell on the floor, where it shattered into a hundred pieces. Suddenly the alarm on her wristwatch buzzed, and the watch began to play reveille. Muttering a curse, she pushed a button to silence her watch, dumped the pieces of her favorite mug into the trash basket, and opened the doors to the shop. Ready or not, she was open for business.

She worked feverishly all morning long, helping customers, dusting shelves, and filling out merchandise order forms. But her determination not to think about Sebastian Gladstone yielded the opposite result. The more she tried to forget him, the more she found herself silently railing at his unfair business practices.

What would she do, what would she say, the next time he showed up? Leaning over the counter, she stared pensively into space. She imagined herself as a princess bedecked in royal purple robes approaching her father, the exalted king of the Persian Empire. "He's wronged me, father," she said. "You must avenge my honor!"

"And what would you have me do, my beloved daughter? Shall we torture him slowly?"

She shook her head. "No, father. I only want justice done. Execute him."

On her order, Sebastian would be paraded before the court in chains. She imagined him kneeling before her, pleading for mercy, knowing his life hung in her hands.

"No, I won't save you," she cried. "Off with his head!"

Sebastian's loud, and very real, laughter shocked her back to reality. She felt the blood drain from her face as she looked up to see him standing right in front of her. How much had she said out loud? She cringed.

"Off with my head?" he repeated. "What the hell is that supposed to mean?"

"Figure it out for yourself," she retorted. "I've got to take care of my customers." Squaring her shoulders, she walked past him in her most regal manner.

Megan deliberately took her time, chatting amicably with her three customers. Mrs. Murphy, one of her regulars, was a jovial woman in her early sixties. Since she had a bevy of grandchildren—one of whom it seemed was always having a birthday—she frequently stopped by for one of Megan's more unusual gift items. Her last purchase had consisted of four bags of Kitty Glitter Litter for her daughter-in-law, who owned several cats. Mrs. Murphy was impressed with the fact that the special mixture glowed in the dark. That way the cats could always find it.

Megan's second customer, Lynn Chase, was a policewoman who stopped by from time to time in search of presents for her several boyfriends. She was a tall, long-legged blonde, and Megan could easily see why men found her attractive. Seeing Lynn browsing through a pile of the risqué T-shirts, Megan exchanged a few words with her before moving on to greet her third customer.

She didn't remember seeing this customer before. Megan introduced herself to the college-age man dressed in new designer jeans. Locks of dark brown hair lay over his forehead as he read over the messages printed on her ungreeting cards.

Out of the corner of her eye she saw Sebastian waiting for her. Determined to ignore him, she stayed at her customer's side and offered to help him pick out just the right card.

Forty minutes later, she had rung up three sales. Lynn had picked out a see-through nightshirt that said, "Cops Do It with Handcuffs." Mrs. Murphy had bought a set of candles shaped like the Loch Ness monster. And her new customer had finally decided on an ungreeting card that said on the outside, "Congratulations on your promotion." The inside message read: "Make mine two sugars, no cream."

After she'd finished with her customers, Megan glanced warily around the store. Sebastian was nowhere in sight. She let out a sigh of relief—then almost jumped out of her socks when he emerged unexpectedly from the back room.

"Oh, good. You've finally got some free time," he said, grinning. "I have a surprise for you." Taking in her obvious surprise, he added, "What's the matter? Did I scare you?"

She composed herself quickly. "Not at all. I'm fine. What's the surprise?"

"I want you to have more time to spend with me, so I've arranged for a daughter of one of my secretaries to come in and help you out on a part-time basis. She's been looking for a job she can fit in between her classes at the university, so I think it'll work out fine for everyone." He hesitated, looking slightly uncomfortable. "I'll pay for it, of course."

Megan was furious! "You . . . you . . ." Hands clenched at her sides, she turned on him. "Mr. Gladstone, I do not need your help. For your information, I am not under any obligation to see you any time the mood strikes you. As for the girl you hired, I suggest you take her to your own office. Do whatever you like with her, but keep her out of my store!"

Sebastian's expression was all concern. "What's the matter, honey? Are you having a bad day? I noticed the pieces of your busted coffee mug." He stepped forward and grasped her shoulders in a prelude to a hug.

"Don't you dare patronize me!" She stepped back, glaring. "If you think that what happened between us last night gives you the right to meddle in my life, then think again! I do not need anyone, least of all you, looking over my shoulder."

"Don't you think you're overreacting?" he said stiffly, his own anger apparently rising. "I was only trying to help out."

"You were trying to help *yourself*. You wanted me to be at your beck and call, to help liven up your free time."

"Megan, you're jumping to unfair conclusions."

Megan's temper grew as she met his eyes in a dark stare. "I made a big mistake letting you into my life, but I have no intention of continuing to do so. I want you to leave my store, right now. If you and I have to conduct business together from time to time, then so be it. But as far as I'm concerned, Mr. Gladstone, you're no longer part of my personal life."

Just then, a dapperly dressed middle-aged man, apparently oblivious to their argument, requested Megan's attention. She smiled tightly. "Can I help you?"

"I'm just having a look. I don't usually come upstairs or to this building at all. The shops next door to the grocery store have all the variety I've ever needed."

Megan was momentarily diverted from her argument with Sebastian by the man's unusual appearance. With a neatly trimmed beard and elegant mustache, wearing a gray three-piece wool suit and carrying an old briar walking stick, he exuded an air of quiet dignity and panache, and looked like an old-world banker.

"After glancing about," he continued, "it appears I was mistaken not to have taken the trouble to visit you sooner. Your shop has some very useful and amusing merchandise. I am very impressed."

"Thank you, sir. We do our best."

Megan managed to keep a noncommittal expression, but she was surprised by the gentleman's purchase, one of the generic love letters. All the sender had to do was fill in the blank with the recipient's name.

"I hope to see you again soon," Megan said with a bright smile.

"You undoubtedly will, young lady." He bowed his head and touched the tip of his cane to his forehead in a formal salute. "Excellence should always be rewarded. I intend to recommend your establishment to all of my associates. Good day."

Megan watched him stroll out of her shop, wondering who his associates might be. Would they all look like they had drifted into the wrong century?

It had taken Megan only a few minutes to deal with her customer, and she turned around expecting to see Sebastian waiting for her. But he was gone. Disappointment and frustration filled her. She should never have given vent to her anger so forcefully. Now he had left, and she no longer had the chance to make him understand her feelings.

But maybe his leaving was for the best, after all. It would have had to happen sooner or later. Better to end their relationship now, when she was only a little bit in love with him, than later, when she'd lost her heart completely.

She had to be strong. From now on, she would consider Sebastian Gladstone part of her past, not her present.

What she needed most was to keep busy. She looked around the shop. There were no customers, the shelves were clean, and she was in no mood to tackle the remaining bills. What could she do?

The words of her last customer echoed in her mind. There must be lots of people who had never ventured into the shopping center or upstairs to her shop. How much business was she losing because they had never bothered to come this way? Sure, the rental fee for her store was lower than for the ones downstairs, since her shop wasn't centrally located. She had always believed her merchandise would be sufficiently unusual to draw customers in anyway. Now, as she considered what she had just learned, she had to admit her theory wasn't foolproof.

There must be a way to remedy the situation, some way to advertise. The problem was money. She just didn't have enough to launch an extensive advertising campaign. The few newspaper ads she placed were costly enough as it was.

Then an idea began to take shape in her mind. Some creativity and a bit of entrepreneurial spirit might go far, she decided.

Four and a half hours later, she was putting the finishing touches on an array of colorful posters extolling the unexpected rewards of taking a trip off the beaten path. She had also come up with an idea for a new service her store could offer, one practically guaranteed to bring in customers—provided she could work out the details.

She was wondering if she should leave the store to tack up her posters throughout the shopping center when

Erin walked in. "You're just the person I wanted to see," Megan called brightly, though her heart sank at the thought that her friend might ask why she hadn't come home last night.

"I was sitting around the apartment bored to tears," Erin explained, "so I thought I'd drop in on you and see if there was anything I could do."

Megan handed her the stack of posters. "Tape these up all over the mall. I want people to know we're here."

Erin set them down on the counter and glanced through them. "These are really cute. I particularly like the one that says: 'Lost? Discover new roads off the beaten path.'"

"Well, I hope they help bring in business," Megan said. As Erin left, Megan sighed with relief. At least her roommate hadn't asked about last night. The back of her throat throbbed with a dull ache as she thought about Sebastian. It had felt so right to fall into his arms, but now everything between them was ruined.

Erin returned twenty minutes later. "Mission accomplished, sir!" She saluted smartly.

"Thanks, Erin, you're a true friend. Now, I have one more favor to ask of you. Can you try to get me some *really* cheap air time at the radio station? I have an absolutely terrific idea that I'm sure will bring in lots of customers if I can get the word out to enough people."

"I should be able to get a discount and negotiate a good deal for us," Erin assured her. "Tell me what you have in mind."

Megan grinned. "You know the little repertory theater a few blocks from here where I watched you audition a few months ago?"

"How could I forget? I lost the part," Erin answered glumly.

"I'd never seen so many unemployed, good-looking actors in my life," Megan said. "I remember thinking it was a waste not to put those perfect bodies and faces to good use."

Erin shrugged. "That's the way it is. Acting is a tough business to break into."

"But I've thought of a way to help both them and myself," Megan enthused breathlessly. "I want to offer my customers a new service I'm going to call Rent a Fantasy."

"Rent a Fantasy?" Erin looked puzzled.

"We'll contact some of your friends in the acting profession," Megan explained, "get photographs of everyone who agrees to participate, and post their pictures on the bulletin board. Anyone who comes into the store can hire any actor or actress whose photograph we display to act out their favorite romantic fantasy. Just to be on the safe side, we'll make sure our clients understand that 'romantic' does not mean sexual. A chaperone will be present at all times. With the rules clearly spelled out, there won't be any misunderstandings, and I think it'll be fun for everyone."

Erin's eyes lit up. "What a dynamite idea! I'll call my friends right away and find out who's interested. I don't think we'll have any trouble getting you a wide selection of both men and women. In fact, I might even include my own picture in the bunch!"

"Fine with me," Megan agreed happily. "What about the air time? Do you think you can get your boss to give us a really inexpensive deal?"

"Leave it to me," Erin replied. "The station manager likes me. I'm sure he'll help. In the meantime, I'm going to the grocery store to restock our refrigerator. It's as barren as the Sahara. Anything in particular I can get for you?"

Megan shook her head. "Just buy our usual fare of canned and junk food. We want to be well prepared for the day medical science finally informs the public that chocolate improves the complexion and cholesterol aids longevity."

"Dream on, kid. I'll see you later this afternoon." With a wave, Erin left.

As the afternoon wore on, more and more customers began to drift into the shop. Megan began to wonder if the posters were responsible for the sudden upswing in business.

An elderly woman told her, "I've never been in your store before, but I must say you certainly carry a wide range of items." She pointed to several soap boxes. "Are these really homemade soaps?"

Megan nodded. "The lady who makes them for me does a great job. They're eighty percent lanolin and are very gentle on your skin. The violet-scented soaps are my favorite."

The customer picked up the box and sniffed cautiously. "I think I'll give them a try."

Megan rang up the sale. "I hope you don't mind my asking, but how did you hear about my store?"

The lady smiled. "I was two buildings down looking for a new purse and I kept seeing signs telling me to come here. I decided to take a look."

Megan chuckled. After wishing her new customer a nice day, she turned her attention to the others waiting in line.

The rest of the week passed quickly. Megan's customer load had almost doubled in the past few days. Though she should have been ecstatic, Sebastian's absence hung over her like a dark cloud. He had honored her request and not stopped by since their last explosive encounter.

That Friday, as she was preparing to close shop, she looked up to see Sebastian walking down the hallway! Her heart leaped into her throat. He looked incredibly handsome in dark slacks and a tailored shirt, a jacket slung over his arm.

"I've got to ta*k* to you," he said without preamble. "All the retailers in this center have declared war on me because of you!"

She quailed. So he'd come to see her on business, not because he'd miss*ed* her. "What in the world are you talking about?"

"Go ahead and lock up shop. I'll wait for you in the back office."

Megan didn't like the tone of his voice. Something was wrong. But what? Steeling herself for the worst, she joined him in her office. "What's up?"

"Do you realize that by advertising your store with posters, you're in violation of the lease? Not only that, but other retailers are furious!"

"Furious?" she repeated dully. "Why?"

"Customers come into the mall, see your signs, and, instead of spending their time at the other establishments, head straight for your store. The rest of the shopkeepers claim you're cutting into their business."

"They must be exaggerating, Sebastian. Besides, I'm not doing anything wrong. I'm just being a little aggressive in an effort to increase my walk-in trade."

"It has to stop, Megan. If I let you get away with this, the other retailers will want to start putting up signs, too. In no time at all, each building would resemble New York City subway walls."

"I can't believe this!" Megan cried. "You're not content to muddle up my personal life. Now you're interfering with my business! I'm trying to make an honest profit—which, of course, you'd share in. But instead of helping, you're determined to make things as difficult for me as you can. Surely you know me well enough to realize I wouldn't knowingly violate my lease or purposefully hurt the other store owners!" She caught her breath. "This is just further proof of how little I know you," she added.

"After what we shared the other night, I thought we understood each other very well," he said huskily.

"Don't you dare remind me of that!" she exclaimed. "I prefer to forget past indiscretions. You really had me fooled. I thought you cared about me." She paused, seething with blind outrage. "I was dumb enough to think we had something special going between us. I thought I could trust you! Talk about being wrong!"

Sebastian's body tensed. Anger vibrated between them. "Megan, I have a business to run. My decision has nothing to do with you personally. You mean a lot to me, but that doesn't mean I'll take your side whether or not I think you're right."

"That's terrific." She shook her head. "I don't know what your idea of caring is, but to me it means genuinely being concerned for the other person's welfare. It doesn't mean taking advantage of them. Ever!" She felt her throat constrict. Horrified to feel tears imminent, she fell abruptly silent, struggling for control. She was going to be adult about this if it killed her.

"Megan, I haven't got the vaguest idea what you're talking about," Sebastian protested. "You can't be this upset simply because I'm asking you to take those signs down! I think you'd better tell me what's really going on."

"Sebastian, I trusted you. I believed everything you said. Then I discovered that some of the things you'd told me weren't true. Now I can't help but wonder how many other things you deliberately distorted. Do you feel anything for me at all, or are you simply playing a game?"

"You accuse me of being a liar, then ask for an explanation?" His tone was incredulous, his voice sharp with anger. An ominous stillness fell as he faced her, scarcely moving a muscle.

She studied his unyielding expression. "You did not tell me the truth," she repeated. "I want an explanation."

"When did I lie to you?" he countered stiffly.

"You told me you'd raised our rent because you needed the extra income. Next thing I knew, you had so much money to spare you were giving it away! Yet you knew how hard I'm struggling to make ends meet. How can you tell me I'm special to you and still do something like that to me?"

"The money I donated to the college provided my electronics firm with a substantial tax break. Had I not made a charitable contribution, most of it would have gone to the government. Rather than hand it over to Uncle Sam, I decided to have some say as to how it was spent."

"You're avoiding the issue." Silence stretched tautly between them. "Do you deny that you lied about the current state of your finances?"

"I never lied to you. I told you that, in comparison to what I could have had by staying in the family's business, I wasn't as wealthy. And that's the plain, unvarnished truth. I raised the rent on the mall because I needed to increase my gross profit. Otherwise I was going to start losing money on the shopping center. My electronics firm is doing fine, but if I start taking money from it to help the shopping center, I'll be, in essence, borrowing against my corporation's assets. If an emergency comes up and I need money to tide me over, I won't have any collateral. I could end up losing everything I have.

"I'm not trying to run people out of business, Megan," he went on. "Quite the opposite. The extra money from the rent increase will go right back into the shopping center in the form of advertising. The campaign I'm planning is going to be expensive, but we'll all profit from it. The shop owners will get more customers, and I'll increase my profits. The center will become a solid business venture. Yes, it will be difficult for some of the store owners, those like you, who operate on a strict budget. But their inconveniences now will mean greater profits later. You'll see. In a few months, you'll be glad I'm handling things this way."

"I doubt it," she retorted bleakly. "I may not even be around in six months. But with your cavalier attitude toward money, I'm sure that prospect doesn't bother you. What's the worth of one woman's dream? Not much." She paused. "You have no idea of the hardships you've caused. I still think you could have used the money you gave away to tide the mall over for a few months."

"It would have been bad business. If I used it as you suggest, I would have been simply transferring funds. And I still would have had to pay much higher taxes."

She refused to capitulate easily. "The point is that you have a lot of money, enough to do whatever you please. So how can you raise my rent when you know I can barely afford it?"

"Back to that, are we?" Restlessly he circled her office. "If you didn't want me to take part of your profits, you shouldn't have offered them to me. As far as I'm concerned, you made me a legitimate business offer, and I accepted it."

Anger swelled inside her, partly because she knew he was right. Her pride stung. It was so unfair! "I find your disregard for other people's troubles very upsetting," she said at last.

He straddled a chair in front of her. "Megan, I'm a businessman. The object of my work is to make a profit. I won't apologize for that." He ran a hand through his hair, leaving it tousled. "But you're wrong about me if you think I'm insensitive to other people. I *am* a tough businessman, but I've never dealt unfairly with anyone."

Megan couldn't meet his eyes. She crossed to the other side of the room, fighting the attraction that, even now, drew her to him. "What you're saying may be right," she said thoughtfully, "but it doesn't *feel* right. I'm too personally involved. It's not good."

"You're just trying looking for excuses to avoid making me part of your life. I think you're falling in love with me, Megan Lord, and it scares the hell out of you."

She whirled around. "And what if it does!" she challenged. "From what I've seen of love, it's not an emotion I'm dying to experience. My husband loved me, and kept me in a prison I thought I'd never be free of. My aunt loved me, and used it to justify running my life. Now you come along. The next thing I know, you're hiring a clerk to help me out, then ordering me to take down all my posters, and in general telling me what I can and can't do. Can you blame me for being a little apprehensive?" She returned to her desk, clutching the edge. "So maybe I *did* jump to conclusions, and maybe I *was* looking for excuses, but, darn it, I'm just not ready to be involved with you!"

His expression softened. "I'm sorry, Megan. I know I'm pushing you, but only because I'm falling in love with you, and I hope you'll share my feeling." He paused thoughtfully. "You say you want to grow. Well, often growth is painful. I think that's what you're feeling now. Give it time, Megan. Give us both time."

She let out a soft breath. "I just don't know, Sebastian."

He tilted his head to one side and regarded her warmly. "Can we try again?"

She shook her head. "I don't know...Maybe...I guess so."

Laughing lightly, he caught her in a swift, fierce embrace. "Good. Now, how about dinner? I promised you lunch at a fancy restaurant, but will you settle for dinner instead?"

"I *am* starved," she admitted. "We haven't had any decent food in the house for days."

"My poor, starving love," he murmured. "I'll be happy to fill you up. But how about if I help you take down the posters first?"

She frowned. "If we have to." At his warning look, she added, "Oh, all right." He reached for her coat, but she stayed his arm. "Thanks for offering to help, Sebastian."

He shrugged. "What are . . . friends for?" He bent close to her ear. "Lovers, too."

As they headed out the door, Megan felt happier than she had in days.

CHAPTER SEVEN

DURING THE WEEK that followed, Sebastian was away on a business trip. Megan vacillated between missing him and being glad he was gone. More than once, she caught herself fantasizing about him. She was Scarlett O'Hara, and a Union soldier had just insulted her honor. Sebastian, as Rhett Butler, defended her valiantly and pledged his undying love. "I will champion your cause and defend you with my dying breath," he promised, sweeping her into his arms.

Nevertheless, Megan's doubts had reasserted themselves, and she'd convinced herself once again that no good could come of their relationship. One way or another, she had to put an end to it.

Trying not to think about Sebastian at all, she focused all her energy and attention on her Rent a Fantasy project. She had to work out a lot of details. First she had to negotiate the actors' fees. Next, she had to hire chaperones. Then she had to arrange to rent costumes at a discount. Erin suggested she contact the company that usually provided the repertory theater with outfits. Megan did just that—and was pleased with the deal she struck. She also made arrangements with the theater itself to rent any additional costumes and, more important, the props she was sure to need. As, step by step, she grew closer to realizing her concept, a feeling of exhilaration took hold of her.

Next, with Erin's help, she launched her advertising campaign. The disc jockey at Erin's station had agreed to plug Off the Beaten Path's new service at an almost unheard-of low price. Of course, five in the morning wasn't exactly prime time, but somebody would be listening. Within days, Megan's phone began ringing and didn't stop. Soon Rent a Fantasy was booked four weeks in advance.

Ten days after she'd last seen Sebastian, she was rearranging the actors' photographs on the bulletin board when she heard someone walk into the shop. Smiling automatically, she turned around and was caught in a crushing embrace. "Hello, Megan," a familiar voice murmured. "I've missed you, sweetheart."

"Sebastian!" Her heart began to hammer wildly. "You're back." As he caressed her hair lightly, she felt her knees begin to weaken.

"What have you been up to while I was away?" he asked.

"Oh, this and that." She shook her head, struggling to think straight in his overwhelming presence. "My Rent a Fantasy project is starting this week. We're already booked a month in advance!"

"That's great," he exclaimed, hugging her tightly. "You can tell me all about it over dinner. We'll go someplace really nice and just relax and enjoy each other's company."

Megan stiffened in his arms. Immediately sensing her change in mood, Sebastian loosened his hold, and she slipped out of his embrace. She took a deep breath. She'd made up her mind not to go out with him anymore, and she'd better start putting that resolution into practice right now. "Sebastian, I've decided it's best if we don't see each other," she heard herself say. "I know I've said this before and then changed my mind, but this time I mean it. I've had time to think things over, and I've come to the conclusion that we have to break things off now, before we create all sorts of problems for each other."

To her surprise, Sebastian seemed hardly at all disturbed by her news. "Are you sure about this?" he asked seriously. She studied him carefully. Did she detect a glimmer of amusement in his eyes? No, it couldn't be.

"I'm sure," she answered solemnly.

He sighed. "Then I guess it's all settled."

"I guess so."

He shifted restlessly and stared down at the floor. "I'd better be going then. Good luck with your Rent a Fantasy. I'm pleased it's doing so well."

"Thank you."

"Your clients can pick the actor or actress from any of the faces here in the store?"

"That's right."

"Then I'd like to sign up for tomorrow."

Her mouth dropped open. He expected *her* to fix him up with a date? "You can't be serious," she protested.

"I am."

"Well, it's impossible. None of these actresses are your type."

"Jealous?" he asked casually.

"Hardly." She stormed over to the cash register. "I already told you, we're booked four weeks in advance."

"Wait a minute," he said, one hand on his hip, the other gesturing. "Let's get this perfectly straight. You said I could pick from any of the faces you have here at the store."

"That's right," she agreed with exaggerated patience. "And all the actresses are booked. Sorry."

"But I don't want an actress for my fantasy. I want *you.*"

"Me?" Her voice rose slightly. "I'm not part of the program."

"You said I could pick *any face*. Well, here you are, and there's your lovely face." His eyes danced with devilish merriment. "I'm picking you."

"No way!" She disappeared behind the counter, making a show of rearranging the paper bags. "Besides," she called up to him, "I don't have a chaperone available, and that's an essential part of the agreement."

"Don't tell me you're afraid of being alone with me," Sebastian scoffed. "After all we've been through together? Wait, wait. I think I've got it. You're afraid I'll convince you to keep seeing me."

"Of course not." She jumped up, her arms full of bags. "I hate to disappoint you, but you don't have that much influence over me. I can handle you without any problem."

"Then what's the trouble?"

"It's simply impossible," she retorted flatly. "I can't take time away from the store."

"But my fantasy begins in the evening...and continues until who knows when." She began to argue, but he held up his hands to silence her. "Oh, well, if that's the way you feel, who am I to change your mind? I know that, despite all your take-charge daydreams, you're still afraid I'll end up controlling you, and that you'll end up liking it."

The bags slid from her arms. Of all the chauvinistic . . . ! "You're out of your mind."

"Sure," he said in a placating tone. "Well, at least you know your limitations. Maybe you do need a chaperone around me. So long. I'll see you later." He turned and began walking out of the shop.

"Hold it!" she shouted. To walk away from a challenge like this one required more discipline than she possessed. Besides, she needed the money. Business was up, but she could hardly afford to turn down a firm sale. "I've changed my mind. Since I did say you could pick from any face you saw here in the store, I feel honor-bound to provide you with the fantasy of your choice."

"You're sure now? I wouldn't want to force you to do anything you didn't want to do."

"Yes, I'm sure," she said testily. Now she was sure he was teasing her.

"Good," he said. "Do you provide costumes?"

"I've arranged to rent them from a local costume company. If I can't find what's needed there, I can get it from the repertory theater's stock. Of course, I have to charge you an extra fee."

"Fine. I'll be glad to pay whatever it costs."

She braced herself. "What's your fantasy?"

He grinned lazily. "I want you to dress up as Scarlett O'Hara, and I'll go as Rhett Butler."

The air left Megan's lungs in a whoosh. Her knees buckled, and she leaned against the cash register for support. How could he know that she had been imagining a similar scenario all week? "What?" she asked dully.

"I want you to play the part of Scarlett O'Hara *after* she's married Rhett Butler and is afraid she's going to lose him. She knows that Rhett is getting ready to walk

out on her, and she's determined to persuade him to stay."
He held her eyes in a penetrating, spine-tingling gaze.
"In other words, darling, I want you to play the part of
a woman madly in love with a man she will lose unless
she recaptures the spark of their love."

For several moments Megan was unable to utter a
sound. She couldn't possibly play out this fantasy! Sebastian had tricked her into behaving just as he wanted
her to act toward *him!* She had to think of a way out.
"Renting a fantasy isn't cheap, you know," she said.
"Are you sure this is worth it to you?"

"Oh, it's worth it, all right. There's no doubt in my
mind about that."

She sighed, defeated. "When would you like this
scheduled?"

"Tomorrow night at seven."

She was about to tell him that was impossible, but
then she stopped. She might as well get it over with
quickly, rather than give herself a nervous breakdown
by thinking about it for a week. "Fine," she said.

He started toward the door. "By the way," he added
casually, "remember that our fantasy starts *after* Scarlett
and Rhett are married. She's not fighting to keep her
boyfriend; she's fighting to keep her husband, with whom
she's passionately in love."

Megan shuddered. How could she possibly go through
with this ruse when she was trying to end their relationship? Then new determination gripped her. She leveled
her best stare at him. "First of all, Mr. Gladstone, it's
not *our* fantasy, it's *yours*. Second, I should warn you
that none of our Rent a Fantasies include any, shall we
say, fringe benefits."

He remained undaunted. "See you tomorrow night,
Scarlett." The roguish twinkle in his eyes made her heart
leap to her throat. In dismayed silence, she watched him
walk out the door.

CHAPTER EIGHT

MEGAN ARRANGED FOR Sebastian's costume and the necessary props to be delivered to his town house. Unpacking her own costume, she asked Erin, "Why did I let myself be talked into this?"

"Simple. You need the money, kiddo. Maybe you're also trying to prove that your will is as strong as his."

"I hate to admit it, but his remark about his dominating me and me liking it really got to me. Can you believe he actually said that? I almost choked!"

"So you're out to test yourself."

"I guess I am. I know I don't want to continue dating him. Now I've got to see if I'm strong enough to carry it through."

"Megan, I just don't understand why you insist on calling off your relationship. I know you like him." Erin sat down on Megan's bed, tossed her long black hair over her shoulders, and stretched like a lazy cat.

"The problem is, I'm too attracted to him, and that's bad for my peace of mind. Now, I really don't want to talk about it anymore. I have to get ready."

She stood in front of the mirror, holding the costume up in front of her. It was an exact replica of a dress Vivien Leigh had worn in *Gone with the Wind*, in the scene of Ashley Wilkes's birthday party. A breathtaking scarlet silk, it had a low décolletage and a form-fitting skirt and bodice. Very sexy, and very unlike anything Megan had ever worn. She sighed.

"What was that for?" Erin asked.

"Oh, I guess I just don't feel much like Scarlett O'Hara today. Josephine the Plumber is more like it."

"Never mind, you'll snap out of it," Erin assured her.

Megan sat down at her dressing table and began to arrange her hair, using a picture of Scarlett O'Hara played by Vivien Leigh as a guide. "I'm glad I was able to find this library book on the making of *Gone with the Wind*. My hair may not be black, but I can copy this style without much trouble." She stuck in the last pin and studied her reflection. "I don't think Sebastian will mind me appearing without a black wig, do you?"

Erin shook her head. "Actually, I don't think he'll mind at all."

Megan shot her a warning glance, but decided not to comment on her friend's cryptic remark. "Are you going to help me get into that costume? In case you haven't noticed, it comes with enough undergarments to clothe everyone in San Francisco."

Erin laughed, holding up the boned corset. "It comes with armor, too, I see."

Megan slipped the chemise over her head, and stepped into the pantaloons. She stood up and took a deep breath. "Okay, bring on the dress. There's no way I'm wearing that corset."

"You're thin enough. You won't need it," Erin assured her.

Together they slipped the dress over her head and pulled it down to her breasts. Megan tugged. Erin tugged. But the dress refused to go any further.

"I'm smothering, Erin. What's going on?" Megan's voice rose out of the silken depths. "Did we forget to pull down the zipper?"

"I hate to say this, Megan, but there isn't a zipper. And there's no way we're going to get this down past your generous bosom."

"Then get me out of this thing." Several minutes later, after much thrashing and muttering, Megan disentangled herself from the claret gown. "This is the most ridiculous costume I've ever seen!" Megan wailed. "How did Vivien Leigh ever get into it? She wore it to flaunt her affluence after she became Mrs. Rhett Butler. I chose it over the others because it was one of the few costumes that didn't have a hoop skirt. I can't believe it's too small!"

"You still have one hope," Erin offered.

"For heaven's sake if you've got an idea, don't hold back now! I'm desperate."

"I could try to cinch you into that corset."

"Are you crazy? Those blasted things were designed to torture women into submission!"

"Either that, or you'll have to call Sebastian and tell him you can't deliver the fantasy you promised."

"I'd die first," she said through clenched teeth.

"You could go wearing only your pantaloons and chemise."

"Oh, sure," she agreed caustically. "Any more bright ideas?"

Erin chuckled. "Does the corset look any better to you now?"

Megan sighed. "Let's give it a try."

"All right, kiddo, suck in your breath." As Megan held the ironlike garment just under her breasts, Erin began to lace it tightly in back.

"Ugh!" Megan groaned. "I'll confess! I'll tell you anything you want to know."

"This corset's your only chance," Erin reiterated, "but only if I can get it tight enough. Brace yourself."

Megan grabbed onto the bedpost. "Mammy," she drawled, practicing her role, "you just have to get me into this corset! I just can't miss this dinner! Rhett would never forgive me." Erin tugged harder, and Megan inhaled sharply. "Then again, maybe good ol' Rhett can just go fly a kite," she added.

By the time Erin had finished lacing up the corset and tying it into place, Megan had lapsed into pained silence.

Erin stepped back. When Megan didn't make any effort to move, she peered cautiously at her friend. "Hey, are you still breathing?"

Megan took a slow step away from the bed. "I think I'm going to die."

"No, you won't," Erin said, relieved. "Women wore these things for years."

"And they all died young." She walked stiffly across the room. "Next time I put any trash in the compactor, I'll be able to empathize." She stopped back at the bed. "I hate to tell you this, but I can't bend over to pick up the dress."

"Just stay still and let me take care of it." Erin lifted the dress over Megan's head and pulled it down carefully. "I think it's going to work this time." After some resistance at the bust line, the dress slipped into place, fitting tightly around Megan's waist and falling into graceful folds to the floor. Erin stood back. "Wow! You're going to knock Sebastian off his feet when he sees you in this."

"Actually," Megan said thoughtfully, "this corset may be the answer to my problem. I've been worried that I won't be able to keep in control if Sebastian . . . well, you know. But in this corset I'll be in too much pain to worry about him. It's hard to think about love when your very survival is at stake."

Erin laughed. "I have to tell you, Megan, regardless of your discomfort, I've never seen you look more stunning."

"Call a taxi, will you? I don't think I can drive myself over there."

"Wouldn't you rather I call Sebastian? He can pick you up and save you the fare."

"No, I'll just add the cost to the price of his fantasy." Picking up the small handbag that went with the costume, Megan moved slowly into the living room. "I think I'm beginning to get the hang of this. I'm all right as long as I don't breathe deeply."

"Try panting instead. Sebastian might think it's sexy, or that you're terribly turned on, but you can't have everything."

In the taxi, on the way to Sebastian's town house, Megan tried to ignore the driver's blatant stare. She felt compelled to protest, however, when he narrowly missed colliding with a bus because he was looking at Megan's bosom. When he finally pulled up in front of Sebastian's beautiful home, Megan scrimped on the tip—he didn't deserve it!—and carefully extricated herself from the back seat.

Before she even reached the front door, Sebastian opened it. For an instant she thought she might die on the spot, right then and there. He looked absolutely stunning in black nineteenth-century evening clothes. The velvet collar and cuffs of the cutaway jacket matched the black string bow tie. The white, ruffled shirt, covered by a U-cut silk vest, made him look the epitome of the southern gentleman. He was even more devastatingly handsome than she had ever imagined.

He gave a courtly bow and, taking her gloved hand, kissed it.

"You look ravishing, my dear," he said, imitating Clark Gable's Rhett Butler. His eyes gleamed with appreciation. Megan had never felt so beautiful.

She fought an urge to laugh nervously. "Thank you, sir. You are most kind." She stepped inside the foyer, and, accepting his arm, entered the dining room. She tried to look nonplussed, despite his intoxicating nearness.

"I've had our meal catered especially for us tonight, dear," said Rhett. "Since we'll be parting ways, I believe we should share a magnificent farewell dinner."

Slowly they approached the sumptuously laid-out dining room table, next to which stood Sebastian's butler dressed as a nineteenth-century servant. Fine bone-china plates gleamed in the light of numerous candles. Cut-glass crystal wineglasses and sterling-silver place settings sparkled against the snowy white lace tablecloth. Megan breathed in deeply at the beautiful sight, then gasped as the unforgiving corset pinched her rib cage. "It's magnificent," she managed breathlessly.

"I'm glad you're pleased, Scarlett." He pulled out a chair.

Megan tried not to wince as she sat down. Damn corset! How in the world was she supposed to eat anything when she could hardly breathe?

And there was so much food! Sebastian had not stinted in his re-creation of a nineteenth-century formal dinner. As one delicious course followed another, Megan's eyes grew wider and wider. Oysters on the half-shell! Trout almondine! Sherbet to clear the palate, then a huge roast beef served with six different vegetable dishes and home-made bread! Although Megan reluctantly left at least half of each course on her plate, by the time the butler cleared the table, she was sure she'd never move again. "Rhett, can we wait and have dessert in a little while?" she asked prettily.

"Of course, darling. But I must say, Scarlett, you've eaten like a bird. Are you feeling well?"

"I'm fine, Rhett, really. I just have my mind on other things." Allowing a hint of a smile, she rose gracefully—and very slowly—from the table and, taking his arm, urged him out onto the terrace. "It's a beautiful night. Let's enjoy it out here," she suggested.

He assumed an expression of exaggerated pathos. "You know we must part, don't you, my darling lady?"

"Oh Rhett!" she cried, "I don't ever want you to go." Her heart began to beat rapidly. She, Megan, not Scarlett, meant the words! She wrapped her arms around his neck. "Hold me against you for a bit."

He held her gently, his lips brushing her forehead. "Until now, you haven't given me any reason to stay. Are you trying to tell me I do mean something to you, Scarlett? Show me that you share my feeling for you." He leaned down slowly, stopping inches from her mouth, and paused for a breathless moment.

It was Megan who closed the gap. Her lips met his, parting even as they touched. He didn't need any coaxing. He crushed her to him, branding her mouth with his lips and tongue.

His hands rose to caress her bare shoulders as his lips moved downward to her arched throat. His touch left her trembling in his arms. His palm trailed a fiery path from her neck to the soft skin just above her breasts.

But something more than passion had stolen her breath away. "I can't breathe," she cried softly.

"Tell me what you're feeling," he murmured as his hand circled her breast.

"I want you, Rhett, but I can't breathe!" With her last ounce of strength, she pushed out of his arms and stepped back. She stood uncertainly. She felt so funny. And then the world started to spin, and everything went black . . .

Someone was calling her name. And murmuring lovely endearments. A warm hand was stroking her hair and rubbing her wrists. She felt a cool cloth on her forehead.

"Wake up, Megan, wake up," the voice said.

She knew that voice, but she wasn't sure she wanted to wake up. It felt so good to drift along . . .

Her eyes popped open. Sebastian's concerned face gazed down at her. "Megan, are you all right?"

She struggled to sit up and realized she was lying on the sofa in his den. How had—? Then she remembered.

She groaned, and this time succeeded in sitting upright, despite feeling as if she'd been stuffed into a sausage casing. "Oh, Sebastian, I really do want to go through with your fantasy, but if I don't get out of this corset, I'm going to die before your very eyes."

He stared in amazement, then started to laugh. "Why in the name of heaven did you wear a corset? Were you that determined to keep me from getting too close to you?"

She pursed her lips. "Have your laugh. You have no idea what I've gone through for you tonight. This costume was a size too small. The only way I could get into it was to have Erin stuff me into this medieval vacuum pack. Unless you can help me out of it, I'm probably going to be permanently deformed."

He let out a loud laugh. "I think this is my cue to lift you off the couch and carry you upstairs to my bedroom."

She shook her head. "You won't make it. With this dress and everything else I'm wearing I must weigh enough to sink all of Georgia."

"How you exaggerate, dear Scarlett." He bent swiftly, picked her up effortlessly, and headed for the stairs. "Any inconvenience you might pose will be amply compensated for when I receive the exquisite pleasure of undressing you."

His words caused her skin to flush with a disturbing warmth. The solid expanse of his chest pressed against her felt rock hard and infinitely virile. A chill went down her spine that left her feeling weak and inexplicably feminine. Vowing to control those emotions before they overwhelmed her, she shut her eyes and tried to will them away.

When she opened her eyes, they were inside his room. He set her down gently on his bed. "Are you feeling any better?"

"I'm not ill, I'm just in pain," she said, wincing. "And I feel terrible about spoiling your fantasy."

He smiled. "How about providing me with another one?"

She regarded him warily. It wouldn't be fair to charge him for a fantasy she hadn't really delivered. On the other hand, she couldn't afford to cover all the costs herself. "I'll make a deal with you," she said at length. "Providing your new fantasy doesn't involve wearing a corset, I'm willing to hear you out."

"Fair enough." His eyes strayed provocatively over her figure. "But first we'll get you out of this dress. Then you can slip into one of my shirts and a pair of jeans."

"Thanks, I appreciate that." She sat up on the bed. "The problem is, I still can't move. I need help."

"Allow me," he offered, his eyes twinkling. Grasping the gown at her waist, he pulled upward. It stopped at her bustline. He looked perplexed. She gave a slight wriggle, and the gown popped free. He guided the long velvet dress over her head.

The corset was tightly bound over her chemise and knotted at the top. He fumbled futilely with the fastening for several minutes. "This is a little like trying to get into Fort Knox."

"I don't know how much longer I can hold out," she muttered, struggling to get air into her lungs.

"I hate to tell you this, but I'm stumped."

"Try again!" She clenched her teeth. Every time he pulled on the strings, the corset tightened. "I'm either about to have a heart attack, or this contraption is cutting off my circulation. My arms are tingling. Pretty soon my fingers and toes will turn blue."

"I want you to tingle, darling," he murmured, "but not because of a corset."

Her head snapped upward, and she arched her back as he pulled even tighter on the fastening. "Oh, this is terrible. Will you hurry up?"

"The heck with this," he muttered.

Once again the corset tightened, she heard a snap, and suddenly she was free. With a sigh of relief, she pulled air deep into her lungs. She could breathe again! "Thank heavens! What did you do? It sure gave way fast."

"I pulled the rip cord."

"You did what?" She turned to face him.

He held out his pocket knife. "When I cut the top string, your body just sort of mushroomed."

Megan's eyes widened, and together they burst out laughing. "Why doesn't this sort of thing ever happen to heroines in historical novels?" she wondered.

He studied her chemise and pantaloons with growing fascination. "For some reason I feel as if I'm about to seduce Little Bo Peep in my own bedroom."

"That's some fantasy, Sebastian."

"Want to play along?" He grinned.

"No!" Pulling a pillow from the bed, she hit him over the head.

"Oh, you want to play rough, do you?" he said, grasping her arms. With lightning reflexes, he pushed her back onto the bed and pinned her hands over her head. He held her steady. "Now, what are you going to do?"

"Beg for mercy?" she suggested.

"Good thought." When she didn't say anything, his lips curled into a crooked grin. "Well? Start begging."

"Beg, beg, beg," she said with a straight face.

"That's not quite what I had in mind," he said with a smirk. "But since you're being obstinate, I might as well demand my alternate fantasy."

Now she knew she was in trouble. Her eyes narrowed suspiciously. "What is it?"

"I want to keep the basic background the same. You're madly in love with me. I'm about to call off our relationship, and you're trying your best to change my mind and get me to stay."

"Right. Do you want any particular setting for this fantasy, or shall we just wing it?"

A slow, roguish grin covered his features. "I know precisely where I want it set."

"Where?"

"My hot tub."

"Wearing my pantaloons and chemise? No way."

"Actually, I had something else in mind." He lifted her off the bed and, despite her protests, carried her back downstairs to a room she'd never seen before. As they crossed the threshold, she heard the sound of gurgling water and the hum of machinery.

"I can't get this costume wet, Sebastian! It might shrink."

He set her down beside the blue and white tiled sunken tub. "Undress while I tell my butler we won't be needing him anymore."

"I will not!" She folded her arms over her chest. "I am not getting into that thing naked."

"Well, I have to admit I rather expected that . . ."

"So?"

"I've come prepared." He opened a built-in wardrobe

and pulled out something small and red. "Here, this is for you." She stared in dismay. It was a very skimpy red bikini. He raised one eyebrow in a silent challenge. "I checked with Erin. Believe me, this is your size."

"How could you have checked with her? Your fantasy was to have me come as Scarlett O'Hara."

He shook his head. "No. My fantasy was to have you come as Mrs. Rhett Butler. Scarlett would not have hesitated to seduce her man into staying."

Megan snatched the bikini from his hands and studied the two swatches of cloth. "Sebastian, for heaven's sake! A handkerchief has more material than this !"

"If you'd rather wear one of my handkerchiefs, I'll be more than happy to accommodate you."

"Oh! Go dismiss your butler. I'll change my clothes."

By the time he returned, she was already in the tub, the water up to her waist.

"Your top half looks very good in that bathing suit," Sebastian commented, "but don't I get to peek at the rest of you?"

"No."

"Is this any way to charm your man into staying with you?" he asked in a raspy, seductive voice that made her pulse flutter like autumn leaves in a storm.

She had failed to deliver the first half of his fantasy. Was she really going to ruin this one, too? Surely, she was made of sterner stuff. She steeled herself. "You're right." She forced herself to smile pleasantly. "Why don't you come in? The water's fine."

He stripped off his shirt, revealing a powerfully muscled torso. A dusting of dark hair arrowed downward and disappeared into his slacks.

Megan watched, mesmerized, as he unbuckled his belt and unfastened his pants. "Wait, you're not going to—" The rest of his clothing dropped to the ground. She flushed and averted her eyes.

She was unable to utter a sound as he slipped into the hot, swirling water. He edged deliberately close to her, watching her expression with the subtle arrogance of a man who knows that the woman he wants also desires him. Megan sat immobile, her back ramrod straight. "Don't be so scared," he whispered. "Let yourself go, Megan. Put yourself in my hands, even if only for to-night."

What was she supposed to do in a situation like this? She felt trapped, yet exhilarated. What would Erin do? Probably say something terribly witty. Megan opened her mouth, but no words came out.

Her lips were still parted when his mouth came down over hers. "Megan, I need your softness. Don't deny me. Touch me, honey. Show me how much you want me."

CHAPTER NINE

SHE COULDN'T LET this happen! Her will was stronger than this! Megan wanted to push him away, but the vital force that burned white hot in the man holding her had sparked a similar feeling in herself. Still she resisted. "No, Sebastian. We can't do this." Her voice trembled, betraying her inner tumult.

"Don't be afraid of the feeling between us, Megan. It's much too special to run away from. Can't you see that?" His breath seared her skin.

She wanted to be stronger, to resist the delicious promise of his love, but as his lips brushed the hollow of her neck, caution ceased to have meaning. There were no tomorrows. There was only today.

His lips continued to tantalize her as he unfastened her bikini top and freed her breasts. Only then did his mouth leave hers. The warm moistness of his tongue left

135

a blazing trail along her throat and down to the valley between her breasts.

Megan wanted to touch him, to run her hands over him until she had memorized every contour of his male body. She stroked the rippling muscles of his chest, watching with awe and satisfaction as his skin quivered beneath her caress.

"Don't tease me, sweetheart." His voice was raw with passion. "I can't take it."

When her hands slid downward, cupping and imprisoning him in sweet captivity, a low rumbling emanated from deep within him. Her fingers lingered over him in gentle exploration.

"Megan!" With a moan, he crushed her mouth beneath his. His tongue was a primitive explorer that conquered and tamed her. Megan lost herself to his kiss; desire flared through her. She remained motionless as he slipped the scant bikini bottom over her hips. She watched as the tiny flag of surrender floated to the surface.

He took her into his arms and lifted her out of the tub, then placed her gently on the carpet. Cradling her head over his arm, he reached for a towel draped over a chair and spread it out beside them.

His arms around her, he guided her onto it and positioned her beneath him. She heard him groan with unresolved passion as he lowered himself fully along her body.

"Tell me, sweetheart. I want to hear that you love me."

She tensed instinctively. She couldn't tell him that! She shook her head from side to side, fighting the words.

"Tell me," he insisted, lowering his mouth to nibble on the tender flesh at the nape of her neck. He ceased moving against her, holding himself perfectly still above her, waiting for her response.

She wanted him desperately. She couldn't deny him.

The words seemed wrenched from her soul. "Yes, I love you! You're a devil, and I wish I didn't," she half choked, "but I do love you!"

He bent over her, feasting on the ripe swell of her breasts, teasing each rosy peak into tingling awareness. Flattening his palm on her thigh, he stroked her silky flesh as she writhed beneath him, tormented by the throbbing need raging through her.

"Sebastian!" she moaned. Desperately clinging to him, seeking the release only his love could bring, she strove to unite herself to him.

Her surrender broke his control. His knee separated her thighs, and they were one.

Megan lost herself in the exquisite sensations coursing through her. Sebastian's savagely in-drawn breath made her heart dance, and she reveled in the knowledge that she could ignite such passion in him. With increasing wildness she twisted and strained against him, until the world burst apart before her eyes in a blazing, brilliant, dazzling release.

Afterward, she rested, languid and content, like a sleek, satisfied kitten, enjoying the heavy weight of his masculine body on top of her. She breathed in his faint musky scent and took pleasure in the feel of the damp hair on his chest as it brushed her breasts.

He stirred and nuzzled her neck gently, then shifted to one side and tucked her against him. "When I make love to you, I experience emotions I've never felt before. No woman has ever touched me so deeply or affected me so profoundly."

His words moved her almost to tears. He truly loved her. And she knew now, without a doubt, that she loved him.

But as the implications of their love became clear to her, she panicked. Her throat tightened; her body tensed. Oh Lord, she'd done it again—allowed passion to overwhelm her. How foolish she'd been to think she could fulfill Sebastian's fantasies yet remain emotionally uninvolved. She'd hardly put up a fight!

If only that damned corset hadn't almost suffocated her, she never would have ended up in Sebastian's hot tub!

But it was too late for "if onlys." The important thing now was to get away from him as quickly as possible.

Why? She was surprised when the answer didn't come immediately to her.

Nevertheless, acting on instinct, she moved away from Sebastian and sat up. She looked down at his still, lean form and met his questioning gaze. "Where are you going?"

"Sebastian, I came here tonight determined to show you that my will to resist you was as strong as yours to have me. But I was obviously wrong."

He reached out to stroke her arm. "I'm glad you were wrong."

"Well, *I'm* not. I can't go on like this. I'm leaving now."

She started to get up, but his hand tightened on her arm, forcing her to stay. His face was taut with anger. "Megan, I'm tired of your running away. What are you so damn afraid of?"

She wrenched free of his grasp. "I'm not *afraid* of anything, but I *am* determined not to continue our involvement."

"Why?" His voice was hard. He was equally determined to get an answer from her.

"Because you'll make demands on me, like you already did when you hired an assistant for my shop without discussing the idea with me first."

"You're right, Megan. I had no right to do that. But, although the action I took was misguided, my motives were good. I just want to spend more time with you. I did it out of love. And I learned a lot from my mistake."

She fought the warm feelings his reasonable explanation aroused. "All that may be true," she admitted, "but it doesn't change the fact that being involved with you would mean giving up the freedom and independence I've worked so hard for. I like my life now, and I don't want to give it up."

"Megan..." Sitting up, he wrapped his arms around her from behind. "I don't want to take anything away from you. I want to add something to your life—love."

She twisted out of his arms and turned to face him. "All love does is destroy my ability to think for myself. Consider tonight. I probably broke the record for the fastest seduction. Look what happened when Jim Lord loved me. I became, in essence, a slave to his demands." She shook her head. "I'd rather live without love."

He grabbed her shoulders firmly. "You can't compare my love for you with Jim Lord's! He wanted a wife and a mother for his sons. I don't want anything from you— just the chance to love you for yourself. It's a very different kind of love, and it would lead to a very different kind of relationship."

What he'd said made sense, but Megan didn't trust it. Every instinct cried out: Run!

"Megan, you're fighting yourself," Sebastian said softly. "I need you, darling. I love you. And I think, deep inside, you love me, too. Can't you accept that?"

With new resolve she deafened her ears to his words. Standing up, she gathered her costume's undergarments and began to get dressed. "Love is a dead-end street as far as I'm concerned, Sebastian. I don't want any part of it."

"You're treating love as if it were some disease!" he accused her angrily. "It's not a sickness; it's a special, precious gift. And you're throwing it away." He rose abruptly and pulled on his clothes, his movements harsh and impatient.

Suddenly he grabbed her around the waist and drew her to him. She struggled to get free.

"Megan, calm down and listen to me." Raising her chin, he forced her to meet his eyes. "I'm not trying to dominate or change you. I like you just the way you are. But I won't let you destroy the beautiful love we have for each other. Truly caring for another person can be a wonderful experience."

He let her go. She straightened her pantaloons, feeling childish in the old-fashioned undergarments. "You're acting like a child, you know," he teased. Her head snapped up. He'd read her mind again!

It took her a moment to recognize the roguish gleam in his eye. Looking down at herself, she smiled ruefully. "Speaking of clothing, remember the shirt and jeans you offered to lend me?"

"You can borrow them on one condition."

"What's that?" she asked warily.

"That you promise to let me show you that love doesn't have to be threatening, that it can be beautiful and enriching."

"That might take the rest of your life."

"Do you hear me complaining?" He smiled, and for once alarms didn't go off in her head. "Well, do you want my slacks and shirt, or not?"

"Haven't you been listening to a word I've said? It won't do any good to try to persuade me."

"Megan, I won't let you give up on us." He traced the curve of her cheek. "You mean too much to me. To let you go now would mean losing a part of myself. And that's too much to ask of me, sweetheart. It's too much to ask of any man."

*   *   *

Megan scurried nervously around the store, cleaning everything remotely within reach. Two days had passed since she'd been with Sebastian. He hadn't called or stopped by. Several times she'd started to dial his office or home phone number, but something had stopped her. If only she could put him out of her mind...

Who was she kidding? There wasn't a prayer in the world that would make the dull ache inside her go away. She missed him, but pride kept her from picking up the telephone receiver. If he'd changed his mind about her, calling wouldn't help.

She glanced at the clock. Erin would be stopping by soon, and she'd be free to go to the city's merchandise mart. Not that she could afford to buy much for the shop, but seeing what the other stores would be offering customers would provide a relaxing way to spend the afternoon. She was looking forward to it.

It was slightly past one o'clock when Erin arrived. "Hi. I hope I'm not too late."

"Not at all," Megan said, grabbing her purse from behind the counter. "I'll be back around five-thirty. Are you sure you can handle everything by yourself?"

"Sure. But can you?"

Megan wondered at her friend's cryptic comment. "What do you mean?"

Erin pointed at the door, and Megan stared in amazement as a man dressed in the flowing white robes and burnoose of an Arab sheik strode into the shop. "Sebastian! What are you doing dressed like that? Have you lost your mind?"

She had barely uttered the last syllable when he swept her off her feet and into his arms. "I've come to take you to my kingdom beyond the burning sea."

"Put me down!" she shrieked, kicking her feet and flailing her arms in an effort to free herself.

Ignoring her protests, he tossed her over his shoulder.

"Stay still, woman. You are now my captive."

"Sebastian, put me down. I can't leave the store open like this. Anyone could—"

"I'll take care of everything," an upside-down Erin promised. "See you tomorrow."

"You're in on this?" Megan accused as she was carried down the hall. "You traitor!"

Sebastian took the stairs to the lower mall, which was swarming with upside-down people. Customers gaped at them and pointed. Several shopkeepers Megan recognized emerged from behind their cash registers to watch the spectacle with big upside-down grins on their faces. Megan closed her eyes in embarrassment and muttered an oath. This was worse than falling in the pool and losing her contact lens!

Her eyes popped open when Sebastian set her on the ground like a sack of potatoes and urged her into a big black limousine. "To our rendezvous, Williams," he ordered.

"Yes, sir." The butler-turned-chauffeur pulled the vehicle smoothly away from the curb.

Megan angrily straightened her skirt and turtleneck sweater. "That unnecessary display of machismo was embarrassing, humiliating, and unbelievably arrogant! How dare you!"

Smiling, Sebastian leaned back in the seat, thoroughly unperturbed, a picture of cool amusement. "Sit back, relax, and enjoy yourself, Megan. I have lots of memorable activities planned."

"That I believe," she muttered, intrigued in spite of herself, but unwilling to forgive him so easily.

"What do you say? Will you play along with my fantasy?"

"Do I have a choice?"

He shook his head, laughing. "Not really. You're

stuck with me for the rest of the day."

This man was constantly placing her in situations she didn't know how to handle! She had to admit that part of her was excited by the idea of spending what promised to be a most unusual day with him. But another part of her wanted to run away, as far and as fast as she could go!

Her cheeks burned with confusion. "Sebastian, sometimes you mix me up to the point where I can't tell if I'm coming or going."

"Good. I'd hate to think you were bored around me." He edged closer and pulled her against him. "And just how would you describe your feelings for me at this moment?"

She pushed gently away from him. "Like being on a wild roller-coaster ride. When I'm at the top, I'm higher than anyone else; but then I'm plunging down the other side and scared out of my wits. When it's time to get off," she added softly, "there's a sick, empty feeling in the pit of my stomach." Immediately she flushed as she realized how revealing her words had been.

Sebastian dropped a gentle kiss in her hair. His breath felt warm against her skin. "Some of those ups and downs will smooth out in time," he promised. "And remember, until then I'm here to hold you during the scary parts."

Their eyes met and held. Megan felt herself melting under his warm regard. Why couldn't she figure out what she wanted? Just minutes ago she'd been ready to give him up for good, to deny her fantasies about a future with him. Now, as she sat beside him, feeling the pull of his nearness, she wondered if she would ever get him out of her life.

They drove for over an hour, but Sebastian refused to reveal their destination. Only once they'd arrived and Megan stood on an empty stretch of beach, still uncertain as to where they were, did he explain, "We're just outside Del Monte Forest on Monterey Bay. We'll be riding up the beach on horseback." He gestured, and for the first time she noticed a beautiful black roan stallion held by a young boy. "We're going to my private hideaway." He lowered his voice. "I've never brought anyone else there with me."

She was speechless as he led her out toward the waiting stallion. "With me in my sheik's costume and you riding in front of me, we'll make the scenario perfect. You'll be my captive as I take you away to my desert kingdom."

"Some desert." She gestured toward the ocean. "What do you call that—a mirage?"

"A minor inconsistency," he countered good-naturedly. "At least, we've got the sand."

"I stand corrected."

He accepted the horse's reins from the boy's hand. "Thanks. The limo will take you back to the stables. Please return for the horse about an hour after sunset."

"Sebastian, I can't stay away from the store for that long!" Megan protested.

"That's already been taken care of. Erin will handle everything with a little help from a temporary sales clerk I hired for the day. It's all part of my surprise, so enjoy. Tomorrow everything will be back to normal." He paused at the animal's side and held out his cupped hands. "Want a boost up?"

She regarded the animal skeptically. "Doesn't this thing come with an elevator?"

"You can do it," he urged.

She took a deep breath, grasped the horse's mane, slipped her foot into Sebastian's hands, and pulled herself somewhat awkwardly onto the animal's back. "Hey, it feels great up here," she exclaimed.

Sebastian mounted behind her in one easy, fluid motion. "Hang onto me. It's not a long ride, but it's a hard one."

He gently kicked the animal's side, and the stallion sprang forward with a toss of his mane, falling into an easy canter.

The wind whipped through Megan's hair as she leaned back against Sebastian, exhilarated by the wild spirit of their adventure. There was something enticingly sensual about riding with Sebastian this way. She felt like the leading lady in a Rudolph Valentino movie.

They rode along the beach for some time before turning inland up a grassy slope that led to a stretch of rocky terrain. Sebastian automatically slowed the mount. "You okay?" he asked Megan.

"Yes, but I can't imagine where your hideaway is."

He pointed ahead, urging his horse forward. "See that circle of cypress trees? It's just on the other side."

They rode over a thick mantle of yellow wildflowers and entered the group of tall cypress trees. An old army tent, with a roof that had been patched more than a dozen times, loomed directly ahead. A small goat, tethered to a wooden post near the tent, grazed calmly. The sight was hardly what Megan had expected.

At her silence Sebastian said, chuckling, "Don't be so quick to draw conclusions. I might actually think you don't like my place."

"I'm sorry," she said at length. "You took me by surprise. I wasn't expecting anything quite so authentically primitive."

Sebastian dismounted and helped her down. "I don't place as much importance on material comforts as you seem to think. Sometimes I like to get back to basics."

"I remember when I lived in Missouri," Megan said thoughtfully. "There was an abandoned shack at the edge of my aunt's property near Lake Killarney. One summer I went there almost every day to work on fixing it up.

It was very relaxing to be alone in the middle of nowhere, away from ringing telephones and the sounds of traffic."

Sebastian took her hand and led her toward the entrance. "Wait until you see how I've arranged the interior." He lowered his voice to a conspiratorial whisper. "I call it my Harem Hideaway. I designed it especially for you."

"How flattering," she muttered wryly.

"Just pray it doesn't rain. I doubt those patches would hold up to anything stronger than a drizzle. If we get a bad storm, we may need life preservers."

"Great."

He bent over and entered through the low tent flap. Megan followed cautiously. Once inside, she straightened and gazed around curiously.

The tent was much more spacious than she had expected. Several cushions and a thickly padded quilt with an intricate geometric pattern covered the canvas floor. Despite the lack of furniture, the bright reds and purples of the quilt and cushions created a cozy space.

Sebastian held out a two-piece harem costume consisting of a jeweled bikinilike top and pants with sheer legs. "This is for you, my pet," he said, reverting to his role of an Arab sheik.

Megan's eyes widened at the skimpy costume, which had obviously been designed to whet a man's sexual appetite.

"This is going to be an educational experience for you."

"What do you mean?"

"I keep telling you that I don't intend to dominate you. Since you don't believe me, I thought I'd show you how an Arab sheik would really behave. Then you won't have any doubts about me."

"Give me one reason why I should go along with this."

"Since I'm already playing a macho sheik, I don't intend to give you a choice."

She glared at him. Standing with his feet spread, and his arms crossed over his chest, he glared back. "All right, give me the costume," she said. "Where shall I change?"

"How about right here?" His eyes strayed provocatively over her figure.

"Don't push your luck, your highness," she retorted flatly. "I'll go behind the tent. And you, sir—" she challenged him with a bold stare—"stay right here. Unless you want to start this fantasy with two black eyes."

She returned a few minutes later, feeling decidedly self-conscious in the scanty outfit. The top left exposed a generous portion of breast, while the pants rode so low on her hips, she was afraid they might fall off altogether. Trying to cover her bare midriff by folding her arms over it, she stared at him defiantly. "Now, what?"

"Now, my beautiful captive princess, I'm going to show you the wonders of love." He stepped toward her.

"You're going to have a difficult time, because after that phony line I may be sick." She moved backward, circling warily. "Besides, isn't this the scene in which I fight to uphold my virtue?"

He paused in his pursuit to mull over the thought. "That might make it more interesting," he agreed at length. "I'll be free to assert my masculine superiority right from the start, to show you the proper place for a woman."

"That does it! Now, I *know* I'm going to be sick."

He lunged toward her, but she sidestepped neatly around a huge cushion on the floor so that it lay between them. "So much for masculine superiority," she crowed.

But the words had scarcely left her mouth when he dove across the cushion, reached out, and pulled her down. "What were you saying?" he asked, lying on top of her, pinning both her arms above her head.

She looked innocently up at him. "Sebastian, be gentler. You're hurting me," she said softly.

In an instant he rolled away and freed her. "Honey, I'm sorry, I didn't—" Abruptly, she leaped to her feet, grinning smugly.

"See? Brains beat brawn any time," she said triumphantly and backed away again.

He sighed. "Too bad," he said, shaking his head. "I hate to do this, but you've forced me to be tough. Why do infidel females always require such a firm hand?" Feinting to his left, he swung to the right and caught her in his arms as she tried to get away.

"I will not yield. I will fight for my virtue, sir!" she cried, trying to wiggle free.

"It won't do you any good," he countered. "In fact, it might tire you out, which wouldn't please me, since I desire your full attention tonight. I want you to dance for my pleasure as well as hand feed me my dinner."

"I'll do that when pigs fly," she retorted, still struggling.

"If you prefer to stay in my arms," he said slowly, "I suppose I could change my plans..."

"I'll dance," she shot back.

She stepped away from him, trying to suppress the smile she felt forming. "Okay, your royal hindness, here goes."

Making no effort to be either authentic or graceful, she flailed her arms in the air, took several short steps in one direction, and turned back the other way. "I call it the harem shuffle," she said. "What do you think?"

"You've got to be kidding," he said. "I had something sensual and seductive in mind." He walked over to a small tape recorder he'd set in a corner of the tent. "Something to go with this music."

A sensuous Middle Eastern melody filled the tent. The rhythmic sounds seemed to engulf them, transporting them to a far different, more ancient world.

Megan listened for a few minutes. Then slowly, she began to move her hips. She stepped closer to him, and began to dance around him, thrusting her hips toward him, then abruptly away when he tried to touch her. As the spirit of the music captured her and the tempo gradually increased, she danced faster and faster, spinning and turning, moving her hips and torso in sensuous, rhythmic undulations. When the music finally ended, she slowed to a stop in front of him. "Well? Did I pass the test?" she asked brightly.

He stared at her as if mesmerized, desire burning in his eyes. "I think the temperature in this tent just went up about fifty degrees."

She grinned, pleased to see she'd had such an effect on him. "Now, what's this about my having to feed you dinner? We didn't bring any food." She raised a quizzical eyebrow. "Do you want me to try to find some wild berries or something?"

"I'm not willing to chance getting served something poisonous by mistake. I arranged to have some dried fruit dropped off ahead of time. The sweets are in several plastic bags in a knapsack by the entrance."

Megan frowned. "What knapsack? Where?"

Sebastian started to point, then stopped. "I could have sworn I put it here," he muttered. "Help me look around, will you?"

There wasn't any trace of the missing item inside, so they inspected the immediate area outside. "I could have sworn I brought it into the tent," Sebastian insisted.

Suddenly Megan stopped short and bent to pick up a chewed, frayed end of rope. "I hate to mention this, Sebastian, but where's the goat?"

He muttered a curse. "We'd better find her. I borrowed her from a friend to give my Bedouin tent a touch of authenticity."

"Is there any chance she's absconded with your knapsack? Goats are supposed to eat almost anything."

"I suppose she could have put her head inside the tent when we weren't noticing and pulled the knapsack out."

"I don't even know where to begin looking. Do you have any suggestions?" Megan asked hopefully.

"Not a one," he conceded. "We might as well just start walking. If we don't find any trace of her in one direction, we'll go the opposite way and continue to look until we find her."

Just then they heard a soft, plaintive bleating from a short distance away, followed by a shuffling noise. They exchanged quick glances.

"Do you think . . . ?" Without waiting for her to finish the sentence, Sebastian ran ahead and disappeared into a thick outcropping of trees.

Megan sprinted forward, following him into the woods. As the goat's bleating grew louder, she heard Sebastian mutter an oath.

She reached his side a moment later and followed his gaze. The knapsack lay in tatters at their feet. What remained of the contents was strewn in a wide, uneven circle around the still-chewing goat.

Sebastian began retrieving empty cellophane wrappers. "Well, it looks like our friend had quite a snack." He studied the animal carefully. "Too bad for her. Judging by the way she looks, I think she's got a mild case of indigestion."

The animal let out another plaintive bleat, lowered her head, and ran toward him. Sebastian leaped to his feet just as the goat's head butted into his upper thigh, the impact sending him sprawling onto the ground.

Megan stared open-mouthed as the animal turned and trotted nonchalantly back toward camp. As Sebastian scrambled to his feet, muttering darkly, she ran to his side. "Are you all right?"

"Sure. But not because she wasn't trying her best to maim me for life!"

"You insulted her appearance," Megan said playfully. "She was defending her honor. I don't know about you, but us harem girls can empathize with her feelings."

He shot Megan an icy stare. "Don't you know it's dangerous to tease a man in pain?"

"I thought you said you weren't injured." Her joviality was suddenly replaced with concern.

"Only my pride," he admitted.

"I don't believe that for a minute!" she countered, shaking her head. "Your pride is practically indestructible."

"Show some respect, woman," he warned.

She moved close against him. "I don't know about respect, but how about if I give you a hand while you hobble back to camp?"

"Hobble?" he repeated, outraged.

"All right," she conceded playfully, "'how about if I help you get your frazzled, dilapidated body back to the tent?"

"How about if, for the rest of the afternoon, you pretend you have a horrendous case of laryngitis and can't utter a single syllable?"

"But if I did that, you wouldn't have the thrill of matching wits with me," she teased.

"I'll take the chance."

But when they returned to the clearing where Sebastian had set up his tent, it looked as if it had been laid waste by a band of marauding Philistines. The ropes holding the tent in place had been pulled or bitten free.

The tent itself lay flat on the ground. Directly beneath the canvas covering, a moving lump bleated loudly and angrily.

"I vote we let her stay there," Sebastian suggested.

"We can't!" Megan protested. "It would be inhumane. How do we get this thing back up?"

Sebastian ran a hand through his hair. "Give her another five minutes, and I'm sure she'll eat her way through."

"Are you going to help or not?" Megan demanded.

"I'll think about it."

"Sebastian!"

"All right," he conceded grudgingly.

He found one corner of the tent and lifted it several feet off the ground. "I'll give her five seconds to make her bid for freedom. If she's not out by then, I'll assume she wants to make what's left of this tent her permanent—ugh!"

The charging goat caught him firmly in the midsection, sending him crashing to the ground, and dashed past. She halted abruptly a few yards away, turned to briefly survey the damage, and began to graze calmly, oblivious to the consequences of her destruction.

Megan laughed. "I don't think she's vicious," she said, "just militantly feminist. Your sheik's costume makes her angry."

"Great," he muttered. "I'll tell you what. You help me up, and we'll just forget the good Lord ever created goats—and that I ever tried to stage a fantasy out of the Arabian Nights. We'll ride back to our rendezvous point, meet the car, and return back to the city and calm, rational civilization."

Megan was disappointed to have to end their adventure early. She found herself wishing they could somehow steal more time away from their busy schedules. With a heavy heart, she headed back to the tent and lifted a corner. "I have to find my regular clothes. I can't go back dressed like this."

Sebastian tossed the canvas aside and helped her sift through their scattered possessions. A few minutes later, they had retrieved the lost items.

"I'll change behind the cover of those trees," she said, dispiritedly.

When she emerged from the woods, back in her regular clothes, Sebastian was standing beside his horse, reins in hand. "Just leave the costume beside the tent," he said. "I've hired people to come along later to pick everything up."

Nodding, she left the costume on the ground, weighing it down with a corner of the tent, and joined him next to the horse.

Seeming to sense her melancholy mood, he caressed her cheek gently. "You see, even if everything doesn't go exactly according to plan, just being with each other can be fun."

As her eyes met his, a warm, delicious weakness swept through her. Would she get this man out of her heart?

CHAPTER TEN

A WEEK HAD passed since Megan's adventure with Sebastian. Their busy schedules had conspired against them, and although they had tried repeatedly to get together, the number of canceled lunch dates far exceeded the few they had managed to keep.

Although Sebastian's media blitz advertising the shopping center was less than a month old, it had already begun to show very definite results. That, in addition to Megan's own Rent a Fantasy campaign, had resulted in a sharp upswing in her business. For the first time the end-of-the-month accounting report showed a substantial profit.

"I can't believe it," she told Erin. "Do you realize that I've earned enough to do more than just get by this coming month? It looks like it's all finally starting to come together."

Her roommate leaned back in her chair. "What I want to know is what you plan to do about Sebastian. Honestly, Megan," she teased, "if you don't want him, I sure wish you'd pass him on to me."

"Nothing doing," Megan shot back, emptying several coin wrappers into the cash register drawer.

"But if you don't want him, why not let someone else, namely me, have a chance to win him away from you?"

Megan glanced up at her friend. "It's not that I don't want him. It's more a question of: Am I ready for what he's offering? No matter how I look at it, I'm still afraid to get involved. On the other hand, I realize that what we share is really very special, and I don't want to walk away from it. Actually, even if I wanted to, I'm not sure I could."

Since the shop was momentarily empty of customers, Megan gestured for Erin to join her in the back. "Come on. Let's have a cup of coffee. I need a break. For some reason, slow days tire me out more quickly than busy ones."

"It's the same for me at the radio station." Erin followed Megan into the rear office, where she poured the steamy black coffee into two Styrofoam cups.

"So, tell me, what are you going to do about Sebastian?"

"You're like a dog with a bone, you know that? You never let go." Megan chuckled softly, leaning against the door frame to keep an eye on the shop. "If Sebastian really loves me, he'll wait until I'm ready. Real love should be able to stand the test of time. In time, I should be able to judge my feelings more clearly and decide if I'm ready to make a serious commitment."

Erin shrugged. "I wouldn't do it that way, but it's up to you." She leafed through a copy of the daily paper. "Hey, look at this!"

"What is it?" Megan moved closer.

"There's a story in the business section that says Excel Electronics may be in serious financial trouble. They may have to lay employees off because a congressional appropriation, which includes the corporation's payment for work already completed, is being held up by debate at the Capitol. It says here that Sebastian owns that company."

Megan's stomach lurched. "Why didn't he tell me?" she exclaimed. "No wonder I haven't heard from him! He must be under quite a strain." She paused, then added thoughtfully, "I wonder if there's anything I could do to help."

"Why don't you go see him?" Erin checked her watch. "The store's due to close in another hour. I don't mind watching it for you and locking up when it's time."

Without thinking further, Megan phoned his office. After verifying with his secretary that he was home, she gave Erin a quick nod. "He might need a friend right now. Erin, you're a real dear for offering to watch the store."

"It's no problem."

Megan dialed Sebastian's home telephone number twice. "His line is busy, and I can't get through," she said. "I think I'll just drop in on him. If he's working, I'll say hello and leave, but if he needs someone to talk to . . ."

"You'll be there."

"Exactly." Megan grabbed her purse and hurried to the door. "See you later."

She drove across town as quickly as traffic would allow. If Sebastian was in financial difficulty, why hadn't he told her? Had the trip to his hideaway meant as much to him as it did to her? A hundred questions ran through her mind.

By the time she arrived at Sebastian's house, her stomach was tied up in knots. She rang the doorbell.

Moments later, he answered. "Hello. Don't tell me," he said with an air of resignation, "you read the papers too." His dark gray tie had been loosened, and dark circles beneath his eyes attested to more than a few sleepless nights.

"What's going on?" she asked, coming inside. "You didn't say a word of this to me, but it must have been going on for quite a while."

"Last week our people in Washington assured me that the funds would be released and deposited in our corporation's account. We expected the money yesterday. I took it for granted that everything would be taken care of, since I had the personal guarantee of the chairman of the House Appropriations Committee. But this morning I learned the money never arrived. There's been another unexpected delay. My accountant called to remind me that the installment for the shopping center is due in three days. Since the principal is so high, if I ask the bank for an extension, they're bound to tack on an astronomical finance charge, one I really can't afford." He paused and pursed his lips. "You see, in order to help out Excel Corporation, I transferred all the available funds over to that account. I just don't have enough capital left to take care of the shopping center, too. Unless the payment that's owed me comes in soon, Excel will have to shut down, and I'll lose the shopping center as well."

Megan followed him into the den and sat down beside him on the sofa. "Sebastian, I'm sorry. It sounds like such a mess. What happens now?"

"Several of my people are working on it. We've appealed to our congressman, explaining that Excel will have to close its doors unless we get those funds today. The government doesn't want that any more than we do. All I'm asking is that they pay me what they owe me.

In lieu of that, I want the government to secure me a loan."

"I don't understand. Why are they withholding the money?"

"One of the senators involved with this appropriation is an old political enemy of my family. His committee has attached the payment authorization to a bill that he supports. Until one goes through, the other is held up."

"Isn't there any way for you to break the deadlock?" Megan reached for his hand and covered it with her own.

He smiled grimly. "I've got people working on it. I can't do any more." He stood up and began to pace restlessly around the room, his hands jammed deep in his pockets. "There's something else I want to say to you. Megan, when I asked you to continue seeing me, to let the future shape itself, I didn't foresee this financial disaster. If I lose all my business holdings, I won't have anything to offer you." He stopped and faced her. "You deserve more security than that."

She stared at him in shock. "Do you *really* believe I would turn you away and leave just because you didn't have any more money? If that's the case, then I guess you don't really think much of me at all."

He shook his head and met her gaze. "You don't understand. I'm asking you to stop seeing me for a while." His inner torment was etched plainly on his features. "I don't want you to have to go through the hard times that may be ahead for me. Eventually I'll get back on my feet, and then I'll seek you out."

"Oh, I see," she replied sarcastically, walking to the window behind the desk. "You want me around only when everything's going well, like a fair-weather girl friend. That's what your ex-wife was to you, and you expect me to be the same."

"I'm doing this for your own good," he insisted. "I want to spare you the unpleasantness ahead."

"Why do you believe it's perfectly all right for you to come to my rescue when I'm in trouble, but you can't allow me to be there for you when you have a problem? Do you really think I'm so weak that I won't be able to take the pressure? Or is it that, deep down, you think of me as only a distraction, someone to keep you amused? If that's the case, then you certainly wouldn't want me around when you need to concentrate on business."

"That isn't it at all. Why can't you see that I'm trying to protect you?"

"Why can't *you* see that I don't want to be protected? I'd rather be by your side," she countered. "I want to share the bad times as well as the good."

Light dawned in his eyes. "I guess this means you've come to an understanding about our relationship," he said, challenging her.

She stopped breathing, realizing the significance of her own words. "You know," she said slowly, "I think you're right. I *have* come to realize something. Sebastian"—she swallowed—"I love you."

"It's about time you admitted it," he said with a roguish, weary grin. His hands slid down her hips, and he pulled her into the cradle of his thighs. "You'll never regret those feelings," he whispered in a raw voice. "I never knew I could love someone as much as I love you. You are and always will be a part of me, Megan."

With unmistakable hunger, he covered her mouth with his own, his tongue probing deep into the velvety recesses. The tender strength of the arms that encircled her made her senses sing. She melted in his arms.

He held her tightly and finally released her slowly. "I'm glad you came today. I needed you more than you can possibly know."

"You've been going through such a rotten time," she commiserated. "While we're waiting for news, why don't you take your shirt off, lie down on the couch, and let me rub your back?"

"That's the best offer I've had all day." He stripped off his tie and shirt and, naked to the waist, stretched out on the sofa.

Megan began to rub the tightness from his muscles. His hard flesh felt so good beneath her palms. After a few minutes he turned over and faced her. She sat back. "Don't stop. It feels so good," he said quietly.

"How can I rub your back if you're facing me?" she asked.

"You can run your hands over my chest. I'd really enjoy that." He grinned.

"Would you now?" She made no move to do as he suggested.

"Oh, come on. Be a good sport."

Against her better judgment, she began to lightly caress his torso. The feel of the hair-roughened surface sent a shock of electricity through her fingertips.

His eyes burned as he watched her. His growing desire became increasingly evident as she continued her gentle exploration of his body. He felt warm, firm, and wonderful, and she basked in a sense of power as he responded to her ministrations.

Longing seemed to drug her senses as she felt the growing tension in the set of his broad shoulders. When he lifted his hand and covered her breast with his palm, she shuddered.

Their eyes met for a brief moment. An unspoken understanding passed between them.

As she stared into his passion-glazed eyes, she felt herself being pulled under by the compelling spell he had cast over her emotions.

He stood up slowly, walked to the far wall, and turned off the light. Opening the curtains to windows that faced the back patio, he allowed the glow of sunset to illuminate the room.

"Come here," he whispered in a husky voice that made her tremble.

She obeyed the pull of her heart and moved toward him. She wanted him. But even more than the physical pleasures he offered, she needed his love.

The dark burning of desire shone on his face. "Megan, you're the only woman who's ever brought out such passion in me. Sweetheart, I love you so much."

She stood in front of him, hesitant to hasten the pace he had set. She felt his hands on her flesh as he unbuttoned her blouse and unzipped her skirt, allowing them to fall to the ground. The rest of her garments followed. Each time his palms grazed her skin, they left an incendiary glow of yearning.

She tried to contain her own urgency, but the unbearable, aching emptiness inside her demanded fulfillment. Sebastian sealed her mouth in an endless kiss and ran his fingertips over her taut nipples, tracing tiny patterns there until a soft sound escaped her lips.

He buried his lips in her throat, and she reached for his belt, unbuckling it with fumbling fingers. He took her hands and pulled them behind her back, crushing her against him. "We have all night," he murmured. "Let's take our time and make love to each other properly."

He tangled his hands in her hair, pulling her head backward, and her lips flowered open in expectance of the kiss she knew would come. He didn't disappoint her. The slow, deepening exploration of his roving tongue wrenched small cries from the very depths of her soul.

His mouth traveled downward, leaving a moist, erotic trail. A long, shuddering gasp coursed through her as he seized the honey-brown center of her breast between his lips. Then, as if sensing her growing passion, he pulled her down onto the carpeted floor.

"I want to love you here, where I can see the stars reflected in your eyes as you melt beneath my touch." Cradling her head gently in the crook of his arm, he devoured her with his eyes. "My feelings for you are so intense, Megan, sometimes they frighten me."

He caressed her face gently, tracing small patterns on her cheeks, then drawing an imaginary line from her temple to her lips. "I want you to need me as you need air to breathe. I want to become so much a part of you that you feel whole only when you're with me." His teeth nipped her skin in delicious torment.

Cupping his face in her hands, she brought his mouth toward hers. "Love me, Sebastian. I need you. I do want you so much. Let's be everything to each other and leave the real world far behind."

He shifted to one side to remove his slacks, but Megan placed her hand over his. "Let me," she whispered softly.

She stood up and offered him a hand. She unbuckled his belt, unfastened his pants, and finished undressing him. She feasted her eyes on his naked form, then rained kisses over his hair-roughened chest.

Her hands slipped gently downward. Finding him, she tantalized him with feather-light caresses that finally wrenched a deep groan from his throat.

"Oh, Megan! The things you do to me!" He lifted her off her feet and carried her to the sofa. But as he began to cover her body with his own, she shifted to the side.

He tilted his head. "What's this?"

"Lie down," she whispered, drawing courage from his love to make one of her fantasies come true.

Sitting astride of him, running her fingers over the rippling muscles of his chest, she began to tease and torment him, relishing his restless hunger.

"Sweetheart, you're driving me wild." He grasped her

hips, trying to fit her to him. "Don't tease me," he growled. Then in one fluid motion he shifted and pinned her beneath him.

She gave herself up totally to the moment, no longer caring who was in control of whom. Only the lightning sensations coursing through her held any reality.

The night seemed drenched in magic. Each storm of passion was followed by a calm, during which she swore she'd never soar higher or drift any closer to the stars. But Sebastian proved her wrong time and time again...

Dawn filtering through the curtains gently nudged Megan awake. Not wanting to wake Sebastian, as well, she tried to slip out of the arms that had held her fast in sleep. But as she sat up, Sebastian stirred.

"Good morning, beautiful." He gave her a sleepy grin. "Where are you going?"

"I've got to get my things, go home, shower, and change. I have to open the shop at ten." She gave him a quick kiss.

His hands tangled in her hair, and he pulled her back against his chest. "It's much too early. Come back here and cuddle with me a while longer."

"I can't." She wriggled away. "I've really got to go. But if you come by the shop, we can have lunch together."

"Will Erin take over for you, or do I have to share you with your customers?"

"You're crabby in the morning, aren't you?" she teased.

"Just asking a question," he muttered.

"If you come about noon, I probably won't have too many customers. That's the slow time of the day for me."

"All right," he agreed evenly. "I'll try to be there then, but I won't promise. I have a meeting with the bank president this morning, and I'm not sure how long

I'll be in conference with him." He sat up and stretched. "One way or another, though, I'll give you a call."

She watched him. If only she could help ease his burden. "Sebastian, please let me know if I can help. If you want to talk, I'll always be available to you. If there's any way I can borrow money against my shop and you think it would help, all you have to do is tell me."

"You've already given me your most valuable possession."

Her eyebrows rose questioningly.

"You've given me your heart, Megan. That's the greatest, most precious gift of all."

That morning, Megan kept glancing at the telephone, hoping it would ring. But its silence remained unbroken. To make matters worse, it was also a slow day at the shop. Only the interviews she conducted for an assistant sales clerk broke the monotony. In between, she listened to radio broadcasts, hoping for some news of Sebastian's company. But she heard nothing.

A little past noon Erin walked in. "Hello."

Megan glanced up from behind the counter she was rearranging and gave her friend a wan smile. "Hi."

"Boy, do you sound depressed! What's wrong?" Erin climbed onto the bar stool behind the counter.

Megan told her about the previous evening. "I didn't think I could handle a relationship, but I realize now that I love him too much not to," she explained. "I don't think I'll ever be ready for marriage, but I enjoy the sparks and excitement that come from just being with each other. I can't give that up."

"So you want to maintain the status quo. Are you sure he'll agree to that?"

Megan nodded. "He was the one who told me that the love we feel for each other doesn't have to lead anywhere we don't want it to go."

"Yes, but what you want and what he wants..."

Someone came into the store, and Megan looked up. Her face broke into a smile. "Sebastian!"

He was carrying a dozen roses. "Guess what? The government secured a loan for me until my appropriation comes through. It seems that Excel's employees all put pressure on our congressman to do something to get their jobs back. My people came through for me."

She threw her arms around his neck. "That's wonderful!"

He hugged her, then eased his hold and presented her with the roses. "These are for being there when I needed you." He kissed the tip of her nose. "And for loving me."

"On that note, I think I'll offer to look after the shop and give you two a chance to step into the back office," Erin said cheekily.

"Great idea!" Sebastian responded, taking Megan by the hand and leading her away.

"What's this all about?" she asked as soon as they were out of earshot.

"I want to talk with you." He shut the door and returned to face her. "Last night we came to a turning point in our relationship. I'm very much in love with you, Megan."

"I love you too," she said softly, raising his hand to her mouth and kissing it lightly. "I really do."

"Megan, I want to deepen our commitment to each other. I know now that you're everything I've ever wanted in a woman."

"Deepen?" Her old fear raised its ugly head. Icy tendrils of fear sent a shiver through her.

"I love you, Megan Lord, and I know you love me, too." He fished a velvet box from his pocket. "Will you do me the honor of becoming my wife?"

She stared at him in shock, then slowly shook her head. "Sebastian, you know I can't do that."

CHAPTER ELEVEN

HE STARED AT her uncomprehendingly. Slowly his expression grew hard. "I'm sorry, Megan," he said finally. "When you said you loved me, I believed you. My mistake." He placed the box into his pocket.

"I meant every word," she tried to reassure him. But she was determined to make her position concerning marriage clear once and for all. Seeing the pain in his eyes, she impulsively threw her arms around him. "Don't look so hurt, Sebastian. I dearly love you. There will never be another man for me."

His lips brushed her forehead, then covered her mouth with consuming urgency. He crushed her against him, one free arm around her waist like a band of velvet steel. Hungering for more intimate contact, she parted her lips, inviting his sensual invasion.

"Maybe I can still convince you that you're wrong to

fight what's happening between us," he said harshly. "Don't you see that being afraid of this can only mean you're afraid of yourself?"

"You're wrong, Sebastian." She pushed away. "I told you last night that I love you, and I meant it with all my heart. But I could admit that freely because I had taken you at your word. You said we could enjoy a relationship without demands, free to retain our individual autonomy." She brushed the hair away from her face. "Now, you want to take our relationship further. I admit that part of me wants to say yes. But a stronger part says a resounding *no!*"

He sat on the edge of her desk and regarded her thoughtfully. "That should tell you something."

"I feel like a piece of turkish taffy being pulled in two different directions."

He took her hand and caressed the palm, sending warmth down to her very toes. "Marriage isn't always bad, Megan. If two people love each other and if they're committed to what they have, they can make it anything they want it to be. Can't you see that?"

Oh, how she wanted him! But fear held her back. "I'm not ready for marriage, Sebastian. I'm not sure I ever will be."

"Megan," he said, his voice gentle, "I don't want to spend the rest of my life alone. But I also don't put much stock in half-hearted commitments. I want a wife beside me, someone who loves me enough to build a future with me. If your goals aren't the same as mine, then it would be just a matter of time before we began to drift apart. I'm willing to be patient, but I won't wait forever."

"I understand that," she said miserably. "I knew this would happen and that, when it did, I'd be torn in two. But somehow having known it doesn't make it any easier now."

"Megan, trust your own instincts. You know what's

right. What you need now is some time to yourself to sort out your thoughts. I'll leave you alone for a few days, then we'll talk again. I'll come back at the beginning of next week. All right?"

She nodded slowly.

He kissed her on the cheek. "See you then, sweetheart."

She wasn't sure how long she stood rooted to the spot. Erin's voice startled her back to reality. "What's going on?"

"He's not going to let it rest, Erin. He wants a decision from me. He wants to get married."

Erin started to congratulate her, but stopped abruptly. "You didn't turn him down, did you?" she asked in disbelief.

"Not exactly. This little world of mine—my little shop—is something I have some measure of control over. But even the best of relationships has no guarantees. I don't want to make another mistake. I'm afraid to marry him and see myself, the person I've become, regress into someone I won't like at all."

Erin leaned over the counter. "You're my friend, Megan, and I'd hate like hell to see you do something that will haunt you for the rest of your life. This is the most important decision you'll ever make. It'll affect your whole future. Take your time, and consider all your options. But remember: Once lost, love isn't easily replaced. It may come once or, if you're very lucky, twice in a lifetime. You may not get another chance, so be careful what you throw away."

"Erin, I don't know what to do."

"Let me look after the shop today. Why don't you take a walk or go home and think? What you need is some time alone."

"Thanks, Erin. That's a good idea. I really appreciate it."

Megan left by the back entrance to the store. By the time she'd traversed the parking lot, she felt some of her nervous tension easing. The fresh air felt good.

Keeping her pace brisk, she walked down the street. There didn't seem to be an easy answer to the problem. Sebastian wasn't like her first husband, yet the nagging fear of failure persisted. After a few years of living as Sebastian's wife, would she learn to prefer dependence to being self-reliant? Would she regress into the insecure woman she'd been when she'd first come to San Francisco?

Yet, refusing Sebastian's proposal meant facing a life of emptiness without him. The thought was almost too painful to bear. Despite her best efforts, he had become a part of her. She hadn't wanted to fall in love, yet love had found her. What was she supposed to do now? Did she reach out and take what he offered, or would she be wiser to run, and never look behind her?

The next few days went by agonizingly slowly. Each day she looked forward to the evening and sleep, so she wouldn't have to think. Yet sleep proved to be more elusive than she'd hoped. If it came at all, it was fitful and filled with unsettling dreams.

By Monday of the following week Megan's restlessness had become intolerable. Alone in the shop, she paced to and fro. She watched the clock tick away each minute. The unhappiness she felt as she tried to come to a decision made everything seem bleak. To make matters worse, she had waited on only three customers in the last hour. She stared at the empty shop, wishing something would happen to break the monotony.

Her pulse skyrocketed. No sooner had the thought formed than Sebastian sauntered into the shop. "Hello," he said, his eyes holding her in a quick but thorough appraisal. "I promised I'd come back for your decision."

The air became trapped in her lungs. She wanted desperately to tell him that she loved him, that he was everything she had ever wanted in a man, and that, yes, she would marry him. But the words remained unspoken.

"I see." He pursed his lips until they became a thin, hard line. "It's your decision, of course." He seemed to be struggling for patience. "I wish I could make you see that you're making a mistake," he said quietly.

She pleaded silently for him to understand. "Sebastian, I can't give you the answer you want to hear."

He exhaled softly. "Well, that's it then. I've got business in Europe that needs my attention. I'll be taking a plane to Paris on Friday. If I don't hear from you before then, whatever we've shared will come to an end. I can't continue our relationship on your terms, Megan. If I can't have you, then I've got to put my love for you behind me and start over again." He paused, meeting her eyes. "If you don't care enough now, you'll never change your mind."

Megan watched him leave, unable to move or utter a sound. Her heart felt as if it were being crushed. An overpowering sadness descended over her. She felt as if a part of her very soul were being ripped away. Her body trembled so that she became frightened.

She could go to him and stop this insanity before she lost him forever. But her legs wouldn't move. Fear held her in a grip so powerful that she couldn't break free.

She had four days.

By Friday, dark circles shadowed her eyes and she'd lost several pounds. Erin, who had stopped by the store to allow Megan a lunch break, regarded her with growing concern. "You look ghastly, Megan. When's the last time you had a complete night's rest?"

She shrugged. "I'm not sure."

"If you're worrying this much about Sebastian, that should tell you something." Erin finished her cola and tossed the empty container into the trash. "Your entire being is telling you that you should marry him, but you continue to fight yourself. No wonder you look such a wreck."

"Gee thanks," Megan mumbled.

"Have you spoken to him lately?"

She shook her head. "No, not since Monday when he told me he'd be leaving this evening for Paris."

"I'll tell you what. Since you've obviously decided not to accept his offer of marriage, you should try to forget all this. The guys in the repertory company have decided to throw a forties theme party tonight. Why not come with me? It'll be fun."

Megan shook her head. "Erin, I'm just not up to it. I'd be horrendous company."

Erin placed her hands on Megan's shoulders. "Look, kiddo, it'll do you a world of good to go out with a bunch of people. Who knows? You might even have a good time."

Megan sighed. "I think I recognize your tone of voice. It's the one that says you're not taking no for an answer."

"Isn't it wonderful how well we know each other?" Erin said playfully.

Megan capitulated. "You're right. I might as well go to a party tonight. I have a feeling that staying home would be unbearable."

"That's the spirit," Erin said irrepressibly. "With that enthusiastic attitude, how can you fail to have a good time?"

Megan shot her a dirty look. "Keep it up, and I'll change my mind."

"I'll get a costume in your size and take care of the details while you mind the store. I'll meet you back at the apartment later, okay?"

"It's a costume party?" Megan said, aghast.

"Hey, we're going all the way with this. The guys

giving the party are the same actors who've been working your Rent a Fantasy scenarios. It'll be really fun. I promise."

"All right," Megan said miserably. "I'll see you later."

The afternoon dragged on endlessly. By the time she drove home, Megan felt exhausted. Her inability to sleep and eat were finally catching up with her.

As she entered her apartment, she saw several boxes stacked on top of the couch. Erin came out to greet her. "Hi, there. I got you a terrific costume. I'm dressed as a vamp, but that image doesn't fit you at all, so I got something lots more conservative for you."

"What?"

"Go see for yourself."

Megan unwrapped the box. The tan, lightly striped suit with white blouse was cut in a slightly outdated style, but other than that it looked like a regular, though rather old-fashioned, business suit. "Not bad."

"It's bound to be much more comfortable than the Scarlett O'Hara dress you wore."

Megan's heart sank at the reminder of the passionate scene with Sebastian that had followed.

Erin inhaled sharply. "Oh, gee, I'm sorry, Megan."

"It's all right," she said quickly, eager to drop the subject.

"Look, we're getting together for dinner, so you'd better get dressed," Erin said. "The guys are having some food brought in from the Chinese restaurant down the street. Nothing fancy, but it will be good."

"Fine," Megan said, trying to act cheerful. There was no point in spoiling Erin's fun. Besides, she had to get her mind off the fact that Sebastian would be leaving tonight.

Could she really let him go? She still wasn't sure. Shaking her head as if to rid it of disturbing thoughts, she picked up the costume and went to the bedroom.

Thirty minutes later, both women met at the door. Erin looked stunning in a black, low-cut gown. The slit at the side accentuated her long legs.

Megan grimaced. "Next to you, I feel like Rebecca of Sunnybrook Farm."

"Don't be silly," Erin admonished her.

They took Wally the Wonder car and arrived at the repertory theater fifteen minutes later. As they walked inside and down the center aisle, Megan stared at the huge neon sign above the doors of a building front on the stage. The sign read: RICK'S CAFÉ AMERICAN. The name sounded familiar to her, but she couldn't place it. Tall wooden doors flanked by large shutters stood open. Inside, enormous planters with leafy shrubbery stood on either side. A colorful umbrella covered a small round table and chairs to the left.

Suddenly Megan identified the setting. "You didn't tell me it's a *Casablanca* party!" she exclaimed.

"That's the first of many surprises," Erin said cryptically.

Megan turned to look at her. "What's that supposed to mean?"

Erin tilted her head to one side. "Do you by any chance recognize the costume you're wearing?"

Megan frowned. "The costume..." Just then she heard someone approach from the right and glanced up. Sebastian was coming toward her! He was wearing a white jacket, a white shirt with a black bow tie, and black pants. It was impossible to mistake the part he had chosen to play that evening.

"You look lovely tonight, Ilsa," he said to her.

Megan stared at him as full comprehension dawned. "I see. For tonight you're Rick Blaine, the character Humphrey Bogart played in *Casablanca*."

"And you're Ilsa Lund Laszlo." He took her arm and

led her onto the stage. As they entered the skillfully prepared set, Erin disappeared into the crowd of party guests.

Rick's Café American contained several round wooden tables with chairs. Two side exits led to arched passageways where larger lamps and planters hung from above. The subtle lighting cast interesting shadows on the wall. It was, indeed, an authentic reproduction of the *Casablanca* set.

As they walked to the center of the room, a black piano player began to play the familiar theme music from the movie. Megan felt as if she had been enveloped in a dream. Smoke from an unknown source swirled gently around the tables, at which costumed actors and actresses were engaged in animated conversation.

Sebastian pulled back a carved wooden chair and seated Megan at a table. An ornately carved chess set placed to one side showed a game in progress. After he had seated himself beside her, he poured her a glass of champagne. She automatically took the drink he offered, her mind in a whirl.

"I thought if we were going to part ways after tonight, the least we could do was end our relationship in style," he said. "You like fantasies, Megan, and your ability to daydream and romanticize is one of the many qualities that makes you so special to me. So I decided to throw this little party."

Catching the sparkle in Sebastian's eyes, she remembered the heart-rending ending of *Casablanca*. Her stomach began to tighten into knots. She didn't want to lose this man! Not ever.

"I've had a chance to think about it, Megan, and I've decided you're right," he went on. "We're wrong for each other. You don't trust me or yourself enough to make the kind of commitment I want you to make. Neither one of us can change that. Forcing something like this on you would be like forcing a bud to open. Instead of a beautiful flower, there would be only scattered petals."

Before she had a chance to reply, another couple approached, also dressed in costumes appropriate to the setting. Sebastian chatted amicably with them while Megan watched, too shocked to speak. The decision of whether or not to end their relationship was no longer up to her. Or was it? Could she convince him to take her back?

The thought startled her. Was that what she wanted? She felt an answer stirring within her heart. A life without Sebastian would be no life at all. Suddenly she knew that, more than anything else, she wanted to be his wife. Why hadn't she been able to see that love didn't make you lose a part of your being, it simply added new dimensions to life? Without Sebastian she'd never be whole, complete. He had become an integral part of her.

She still wanted to be her own woman, but she knew now that she could also be Sebastian's woman without any threat to herself. His love would strengthen the growth she had already begun to experience. For the first time in her life she was on the brink of discovering the joy and contentment that came from a love that carried the gift of freedom in it.

Megan was aroused from her thoughts as a darkly clad waiter approached them to say that Sebastian was wanted on the telephone. He excused himself politely and left through a side exit. A few minutes later, he returned. Taking her hand, he led her to the entrance of the set.

"The evening flight might be canceled due to approaching bad weather, so I'm going to take the afternoon flight that leaves in another ninety minutes." He smiled sadly. "I'd hoped we could have had a few more hours together tonight, but I guess this is good-bye." Leaning over, he gave her a light kiss. "Even if the outcome is painful, Megan, I'm glad we met."

She trembled as she watched him walk out the double doors. The unhappy ending on the airfield in *Casablanca* flooded her memory. Was she really going to stand there and allow life to pass her by because she didn't have enough courage to take a chance? She moved forward and looked out the front of the stage toward the theater doors. They were just closing behind Sebastian.

The stage was now deadly silent. It was as if time were standing still. People were frozen at their tables, waiting for the next line to be spoken.

Megan hesitated only an instant before running after Sebastian.

She caught up with him in the parking lot as he reached his car. "Wait!"

He turned around, his hand on the door handle, but made no move toward her. "Yes?" he asked.

"Yes!" she shouted. "That's exactly what I wanted to tell you. I want to be your wife. Only when I realized I'd be losing you forever did I understand exactly what I was giving up. Sebastian, I've been wrong. Independence doesn't have to mean going through the rest of your life alone. It means still retaining enough autonomy to remain an individual. I wouldn't stop growing by sharing my life with you. I'd just experience a new, less selfish kind of growth." She paused, out of breath. "I love you! Don't let this end. Please, let's get married."

He looked as if a great weight had been lifted from his shoulders. He grinned. "Are you proposing?"

"If that's what it takes to get you to marry me." She smiled hopefully.

He took her into his arms. "In that case, Megan Lord, I accept."

As she gave herself to him, the many roles she had played flashed through her imagination. The final image—that of Sebastian's wife—warmed her beyond her wildest imaginings. The promise of his love was sweet as his lips descended to hers.

WONDERFUL ROMANCE NEWS!

Do you know about the exciting SECOND CHANCE AT LOVE/TO HAVE AND TO HOLD newsletter? Are you on our *free* mailing list? If reading all about your favorite authors, getting sneak previews of their latest releases, and being filled in on all the latest happenings and events in the romance world sounds good to you, then you'll love our SECOND CHANCE AT LOVE and TO HAVE AND TO HOLD Romance News.

If you'd like to be added to our mailing list, just fill out the coupon below and send it in…and we'll send you your *free* newsletter every three months — hot off the press.

☐ *Yes, I would like to receive your free SECOND CHANCE AT LOVE/TO HAVE AND TO HOLD newsletter.*

Name _____

Address _____

City _____ **State/Zip** _____

Please return this coupon to:

Berkley Publishing
200 Madison Avenue, New York, New York 10016
Att: Irene Majuk

74

HERE'S WHAT READERS ARE SAYING ABOUT

Second Chance at Love

"I think your books are great. I love to read them, as does my family."
— *P. C., Milford, MA**

"Your books are some of the best romances I've read."
— *M. B., Zeeland, MI**

"SECOND CHANCE AT LOVE is my favorite line of romance novels."
— *L. B., Springfield, VA**

"I think SECOND CHANCE AT LOVE books are terrific. I married my 'Second Chance' over 15 years ago. I truly believe love is lovelier the second time around!"
— *P. P., Houston, TX**

"I enjoy your books tremendously."
— *I. S., Bayonne, NJ**

"I love your books and read them all the time. Keep them coming—they're just great."
— *G. L., Brookfield, CT**

"SECOND CHANCE AT LOVE books are definitely the best.!"
— *D. P., Wabash, IN**

*Name and address available upon request

Second Chance at Love®

____07595-7 **RECKLESS DESIRE #180** Nicola Andrews
____07596-5 **THE RUSHING TIDE #181** Laura Eaton
____07597-3 **SWEET TRESPASS #182** Diana Mars
____07598-1 **TORRID NIGHTS #183** Beth Brookes
____07800-X **WINTERGREEN #184** Jeanne Grant
____07801-8 **NO EASY SURRENDER #185** Jan Mathews
____07802-6 **IRRESISTIBLE YOU #186** Claudia Bishop
____07803-4 **SURPRISED BY LOVE #187** Jasmine Craig
____07804-2 **FLIGHTS OF FANCY #188** Linda Barlow
____07805-0 **STARFIRE #189** Lee Williams
____07806-9 **MOONLIGHT RHAPSODY #190** Kay Robbins
____07807-7 **SPELLBOUND #191** Kate Nevins
____07808-5 **LOVE THY NEIGHBOR #192** Frances Davies
____07809-3 **LADY WITH A PAST #193** Elissa Curry
____07810-7 **TOUCHED BY LIGHTNING #194** Helen Carter
____07811-5 **NIGHT FLAME #195** Sarah Crewe
____07812-3 **SOMETIMES A LADY #196** Jocelyn Day
____07813-1 **COUNTRY PLEASURES #197** Lauren Fox
____07814-X **TOO CLOSE FOR COMFORT #198** Liz Grady
____07815-8 **KISSES INCOGNITO #199** Christa Merlin
____07816-6 **HEAD OVER HEELS #200** Nicola Andrews
____07817-4 **BRIEF ENCHANTMENT #201** Susanna Collins
____07818-2 **INTO THE WHIRLWIND #202** Laurel Blake
____07819-0 **HEAVEN ON EARTH #203** Mary Haskell
____07820-4 **BELOVED ADVERSARY #204** Thea Frederick
____07821-2 **SEASWEPT #205** Maureen Norris
____07822-0 **WANTON WAYS #206** Katherine Granger
____07823-9 **A TEMPTING MAGIC #207** Judith Yates
____07956-1 **HEART IN HIDING #208** Francine Rivers
____07957-X **DREAMS OF GOLD AND AMBER #209** Robin Lynn
____07958-8 **TOUCH OF MOONLIGHT #210** Liz Grady
____07959-6 **ONE MORE TOMORROW #211** Aimée Duvall
____07960-X **SILKEN LONGINGS #212** Sharon Francis
____07961-8 **BLACK LACE AND PEARLS #213** Elissa Curry

All of the above titles are $1.95
Prices may be slightly higher in Canada.

Available at your local bookstore or return this form to:

SECOND CHANCE AT LOVE
Book Mailing Service
P.O. Box 690, Rockville Centre, NY 11571

Please send me the titles checked above. I enclose _____ Include 75¢ for postage
and handling if one book is ordered; 25¢ per book for two or more not to exceed
$1.75. California, Illinois, New York and Tennessee residents please add sales tax.

NAME_____

ADDRESS_____

CITY_____ STATE/ZIP_____

(allow six weeks for delivery)   **SK-41b**